"WE HAD SET UP A CLAYMORE AMBUSH . . ."

▼

"Please continue," the lawyer prodded the black soldier. "Remember why you are here today."

"We were just about ready to break down the ambush when this black soldier just walks out of the jungle."

"Can you identify this black soldier? Is he in this room?" Heller's voice was commanding.

"Yes, sir."

"Please point him out to the members of the Board."

Barker slowly raised his hand and pointed directly at James. The soldier's finger shook but he held his arm up and spoke. "It was him."

"Are you sure?" Heller needed a positive identification.

"Absolutely . . . he talked to me and told me to take off after he had shot my squad leader in the back of the head and two more of my squad." The black soldier stood up and his voice rose. "What do you think I am!" He was yelling at James. "They were my *buddies*!"

James sprang to his feet. "They were devilbeasts!"

Barker's voice rose to a scream. "You're the devil!"

"You're *dead*! Do y

ALSO BY DONALD E. ZLOTNIK

Survivor of Nam #1: Baptism
Survivor of Nam #2: P.O.W.
Survivor of Nam #3: Black Market

Published by
POPULAR LIBRARY

COURT-MARTIAL

SURVIVOR OF NAM #4

DONALD E. ZLOTNIK

POPULAR LIBRARY

An Imprint of Warner Books, Inc.

A Warner Communications Company

POPULAR LIBRARY EDITION

Cover design by Jackie Merri Meyer
Cover photograph by Burgess Blevins

Popular Library books are published by
Warner Books, Inc.
666 Fifth Avenue
New York, N.Y. 10103

A Warner Communications Company

Printed in the United States of America

First Printing: November, 1988

10 9 8 7 6 5 4 3 2 1

Hello Spence!

I hope you're getting better. We were beginning to worry there for a while.

The war is still going on. I miss having you watch my rear.

I hear that you've won the Big One! Congratulations, I know you've earned it.

Well, Spence, the war calls.

David

CHAPTER ONE

The Devilbeasts

She hunted by touch in the early morning darkness. A small Ord's kangaroo rat held a sunflower seed between its paws and nibbled cautiously while it squatted close to the base of the tall plant. She walked slowly in the loose gravel that bordered the hot asphalt road, stopping often to touch dead insects with her pedipalps before continuing on her journey. She preferred live prey.

The rat twitched its tail and nervously took another bite from the seed. The darkness prevented the kangaroo rat from seeing her approach, but the small mammal sensed danger. She brushed against the edge of the asphalt and quickly moved away from the heat. The surface of the semiarid desert highway reached 150 degrees during the day and would cool down enough during the evening to attract rattlesnakes. She didn't like the sudden change in surface temperatures and stayed on the gravel near the low tumbleweeds and sunflowers.

The kangaroo rat finished the sunflower seed it had been eating and reached over for another one on the ground nearby just as her right pedipalp touched the brush end of its tail. The instinctive reactions from both the kangaroo rat and the four-inch desert tarantula were instantaneous. The tarantula jumped forward using her eight legs and held her chelicerae open ready to inflict her venom. The kangaroo rat jumped eight feet straight up in the air and kicked out with its large rear feet.

The microsecond advantage went to the small kangaroo rat. If she had touched it anywhere else on its body, she would have won, but the initial contact on the tip of its long tail had misdirected her attack angle.

The kangaroo rat hopped out over the sand and she continued hunting along the roadside, the rat instantly forgotten.

A pale glow started appearing in the eastern sky in front of the Cadillac Seville's hood ornament. The mean-eyed black man behind the wheel glanced over at his sleeping partner on the passenger seat and gave him a dirty look. He continued driving for another five miles and looked over again at the sleeping man. It hadn't pleased him at all to be teamed up with him, but the minister for leadership at the Los Angeles mosque had assigned them together and he could only obey.

The driver nudged his partner. "Wake up. There's a detour sign up ahead."

"Huh?" The passenger had been sleeping so deeply that he woke up disoriented.

"Get the map out of the glove compartment and look for a good road east." The driver pointed at the dashboard.

"Man, I don't know how to read a fucking map."

The driver shook his head in disgust. "Man, what the fuck are you good for?"

"You'll see. . . ." The passenger reached into his shirt pocket and pulled out a cigarette without removing the pack. He used the car's lighter and blew the first lungful of smoke out against the front window.

The driver coughed and reached over to push the switch that opened the passenger window. A rush of warm air entered the car. "Shit! It's already hot out there."

"We were smart driving through the desert at night." The passenger inhaled again.

"We?" The driver flashed his partner a disgusted look.

"Hey, man, is it my fault that I never learned how to drive a car?"

"Hand me the fucking map and shut up." The driver pulled

the canary-yellow Cadillac off to the side of the road and held out his hand for the map. The large orange sign ahead showed that the detour off Highway 40 was south along Texas Highway 287.

"Where are we?"

The driver located himself on the map before answering. "We're just outside of Amarillo."

"Where the fuck is Amarillo?"

"Texas." The driver adjusted the map under the dome light so that he could see the narrow red lines that depicted paved state roads. "We can cut off 287 and take 256 until it runs into 62; that goes due east through Oklahoma, where we can pick up the turnpike. . . ."

The passenger shrugged his shoulders. He was going along for the ride until they reached Ford Leavenworth, Kansas. "Fine with me."

The driver looked back in his rearview mirror and adjusted his wide shoulders against the leather seat. He could feel the tension in his neck muscles from driving all night. "We should reach Kansas by noon."

She stopped walking and raised both of her front walking legs. The soft morning light signaled the end of her hunting for the night. Her burrow was nearby under a free-form blob of concrete that had been dumped on the side of the road by a cement truck when they had poured the foundations for the nearby rest stop.

He saw her and rushed forward from under the overhanging rock he had been checking out for a female's burrow. She arched her cephalothorax and extended her fangs in a defensive posture at the rapid approach of the large male. He didn't pause but touched her front legs with his and then tried scurrying around her abdomen to mate. She turned and maintained her defensive posture, not knowing what his intentions were, but she liked the touch of the male and lowered her legs slightly.

The Cadillac's headlights switched off automatically when the first rays of the sun touched the front of the car.

"Pull over at that rest stop so I can take a piss." The passenger in the car pointed.

"I can use a stretch." The driver eased the car off the road and around the orange barrels that blocked the portion of the entrance waiting to be paved. "It doesn't look like it's open yet."

"Just pull over so I can piss."

The driver stopped the car but left the engine running so that the interior would stay cool from the air conditioner. He stretched and felt his muscles loosen. Years of weight lifting and kick boxing had given him a heavy layer of muscles over his large frame. He was a big man by anybody's standards, but so was his partner.

"I'm going to take a little walk and loosen up a bit. . . . It would be nice if they would design cars for *men*."

The passenger ignored the comment and tried directing his stream of urine so that it would hit a small lizard that was dozing on a nearby rock. He missed by only a couple of inches but a fine spray hit the reptile and it went scurrying off over the sand. The man smiled.

"Fuck! Come here and look at this!" the driver yelled over his shoulder from fifty feet away.

The reaction from his partner was initially centered around alarm and he reached under his loose-fitting jacket and touched the handle of his pistol before realizing that the driver was waving to indicate that he had found something.

"What the fuck do you want?"

"Open the car trunk and get me a box or sack—quick!"

"How do you open the trunk?"

The driver started running back to the car. "You've got to be the dumbest nigger in Los Angeles!"

"Watch who you're calling a nigger . . . motherfucker!"

The driver ignored his partner and reached into the glove compartment and pushed the button that opened the electric trunk. He ran around to the rear of the vehicle and saw that it was empty except for their small suitcases. "Shit!"

"What are you looking for?" The passenger lit another cigarette and watched.

The driver didn't answer. He saw a small box that contained a set of tire chains and dumped out the contents. "What the fuck do they need snow chains for in California?" The driver held one part of the chain box in his left hand and the top portion of the box in his right hand as he ran back to where he had been standing. The passenger became curious and followed him.

The male tarantula had convinced the female and they were mating when the driver returned to the slab of concrete where the two large spiders were locked together.

"*Man!* What the fuck are those things?" The passenger took a step backward and pointed with the glowing tip of his cigarette.

"Tarantulas."

"What are you going to do?"

"Catch them . . ."

"You crazy, man!"

"The minister for leadership in Detroit will like them. They'll make a nice present. . . ." The driver held the bottom half of the chain box on its side near the mating tarantulas and used the top of the box to scoop them up. He slipped the heavy cardboard top over the bottom half and heard the large spiders bump against the sides, trying to escape. The darkness inside the box calmed the large arachnids once the driver had placed the box in the trunk and punched a couple of air holes in the top.

"You going to give the minister . . . *spiders* for a present?" The passenger looked scared.

"He likes that kind of stuff . . . but first we've got some work to do." The driver nodded and they got back into the car.

The olive drab military sedan was parked in front of the gate leading into the Federal Correction Facility at Fort Leavenworth, Kansas. The rear doors of the vehicle were open and the driver stood next to the closed gate holding a riot shotgun with its butt on his hip and its barrel pointed up in the air. The driver was bored. He had been waiting for over an hour for the interior guards to deliver the prisoner so that he could drive them over to the airstrip.

A door opened on the side of the long building and a captain accompanied by two military policemen exited the narrow doorway followed by a single prisoner wearing unironed military fatigues and lightweight waist and leg chains. A single MP carrying a shotgun brought up the rear of the routine prisoner-transfer procession.

The military policeman waiting by the main gate sighed when he saw the prisoner exit the building. He wanted to get the detail over with so that he could pick up his girlfriend and spend the afternoon water skiing on Perry Lake. He lowered his shotgun and looked up at the tower; the guard on duty there had his back toward him and it looked like he was dancing with himself. The MP driver pushed the buzzer switch that was mounted on the fence next to the gate.

The duty MP in the tower heard the sound of the buzzer over the music that was blaring in his ears from his Sony Walkman. He pulled off the headset and looked down at the gate and smiled when he saw that it was only an enlisted MP. He had been warned by the captain that if he was caught again listening to music while he was on duty, he would be given an Article 15.

The tower guard reached over and pushed the intercom switch. "Yeah?"

"The captain is bringing out that motherfucking traitor." The driver nodded back toward the administration wing of the prison.

The tower guard turned so that he could look back down the long sidewalk. "Thanks, man . . ."

"You're not listening to your tape player again, are you?" The detail driver's voice was filled with resignation. "What's it going to take for you to learn a fucking lesson?"

"It's *boring* up here!" The young MP could hear the music coming from the headset hanging around his neck and did a quick dance step. "I can't handle it without something to pass the time away!"

"Well, you'd better hide that headset or the captain will nail your ass!"

"Can you see it from down there?"

"I wouldn't have told you to hide it if I couldn't!" The MP driver looked over at his sedan to make sure that it was parked in the right spot and everything was set up according to regulations. He didn't want the captain to ride his ass. "And you'd better get your ass out on the catwalk before he gets here! Damn, man! You'd better start waking up or the captain will transfer your skinny ass over to maximum security for duty, where the guards suffer *more* than the prisoners!"

The MP driver made sense. The tower guard released the talk button, hurried to hide his Walkman, and removed his M-16 from its rack. He looked over at his ammunition belt and decided that he had better put the damn thing on or the captain would ride his ass. The heat outside the air-conditioned tower would already be up to the sweating level even though it was still early in the morning. He opened one of his ammo pouches and removed one of the twenty-round magazines. Regulations didn't allow for a magazine to be inserted into a weapon unless there was probable cause for that kind of precaution. He looked over at the approaching officer and decided to break up the boredom by inserting a magazine into his M-16, then he smiled to himself and pulled back the charging handle, chambering a round. He felt the excitement growing and flipped off the safety switch using his thumb. His M-16 was fully loaded and ready to fire at the slightest pull from his index finger. He felt the adrenaline rushing to his head as he placed the butt end of his rifle on his right hip and walked around the catwalk until he was standing directly over the fence. A weatherproofed switch had been installed on the railing so that the tower guard could ensure that the area surrounding the gate was clear before opening it for visitors or for exiting prisoners.

The two black military policemen stepped out from behind the building a hundred meters away from the fence. They had been waiting since dawn for the prisoner to be moved out to the waiting military sedan. The driver of the canary-yellow Cadillac glanced over at his partner, who was dressed in an identical set of military fatigues, and smiled. He reached over with his right hand and adjusted his black armband with the large white MP letters and then started walking fast to intersect the prisoner party before they reached the waiting sedan. Only a very close inspection of the two black MPs would reveal that they carried fourteen-round Browning 9mm pistols in their government-issue holsters instead of the U.S. Army

.45s that they were supposed to carry; everything else about their uniforms was perfect.

The captain started looking up at the tower guard as he neared the gate but then his attention was drawn to the approaching pair of MPs. The tower guard felt the excitement in his stomach as the captain drew closer. The magazine stuck out from the receiver of his M-16 like a telephone pole and appeared to be growing longer the closer the captain got to the tower. He was starting to think that it might not have been such a good idea to screw with the captain, but it was too late to try to remove the magazine from his weapon.

The captain stopped at the gate and noticed that the two black MPs had slowed down. He didn't like the way they were acting and noticed that they didn't carry their M-16s as though they were comfortable with them. He glanced up at the tower guard and noticed instantly that the MP had a magazine inserted in his weapon. The captain clenched his jaws. He had just taken the last straw from the young soldier. The man was way too immature to work the prison. He had told the colonel that all the military policemen assigned to the federal prison should be at least twenty years old. The civilian captain for the federal guards had complained already about the young soldier's conduct while on duty. The captain didn't have to try to guess whether the magazine was full—he *knew* the kid was dumb enough to use a full magazine. He probably even had a round in the chamber! The captain gave the tower guard a quick, threatening glare; if that kid had a round in the chamber of his weapon, he was going to personally shoot the dumb bastard!

The approaching MPs again drew the captain's attention away from the tower guard. Something was wrong. He reached up and laced his fingers through the Cyclone fence and held the palm of his right hand out to stop the MPs escorting the prisoner.

"Hold the prisoner right there until I check something out." The escort MPs obeyed. The captain then glanced up at the tower guard. "Hit the buzzer and let me out."

The tower guard felt his stomach roll. He knew that the captain had seen the magazine in his weapon, just by the tone in the officer's voice. "Yes sir!"

The huge black MP sensed that something was going wrong when he saw the captain hold up his hand and stop the prisoner. He looked over at his partner and whispered, "The gate is open. We've got to take them out *now* if that fucking captain suspects us . . . hear!"

The other black MP nodded and slipped his thumb along the receiver of his M-16 and pushed against the safety.

The captain saw the slight movement of the man's thumb as he approached the pair. He started dropping down into a squat and pointed at the two men with his left hand. *"Hold it right there!"* He reached for his .45 with his right hand as the bigger black MP lowered the barrel of his M-16 and fired.

The captain took a round high up in his left shoulder and spun around from the impact. The second black MP fired at the MP driver and killed him before he knew what was going on. The driver's body caught the edge of the open gate as he fell and started it moving toward the electric lock.

"Stop that gate!" the black driver screamed at his partner, who was closer to the closing gate.

The prisoner saw the gate closing and started hobbling toward it. He knew that his guards were carrying empty weapons and it would take them a couple of minutes to load their shotguns. Regulations at the federal prison stated that all guards would carry ammunition on their person, but not loaded in the weapons unless there was an actual threat to their persons. A dumb regulation.

The tower guard heard the black MP screaming and saw the prisoner hobbling toward the closing gate. He raised his M-16 to his shoulder and fired a short burst at the thick steel frame. The impact from the rounds slammed the gate shut just as the prisoner's fingers clawed the mesh steel. The tower guard switched his attention to the surprised pair of black MPs; they had been told that the guards didn't carry loaded weapons. The second burst from the tower guard's M-16 ripped across the chest of the black man who stood closest to the gate. The other black man fired up at the catwalk, sending sparks flying when his rounds impacted the steel frame.

The escort MPs had loaded their weapons and began returning fire. The black phony military policeman realized that there was no way he could break through the fence and take the prisoner with him. He had failed, so now it was only a matter of trying to save his own life. He fired as he ran back across the open asphalt parking area. The MPs inside the prison compound returned his fire, but most of their rounds were deflected by the Cyclone fence. The tower guard dropped down on one knee and changed magazines. He was the only one who had a clear shot at the escaping man.

One of the escort MPs ran forward and shoved the hot barrel of his shotgun against the prisoner's neck. "Make *one* move, James, and I'll blow your shit away!"

"I ain't going anywhere . . . honkie!" The prisoner spit out the words. He was more pissed at his brothers who had screwed up his escape than at the MP holding the burning barrel against his neck.

The tower guard threw his M-16 to his shoulder and fired a wild volley at the escaping phony MP. The black man slipped around the corner of the building just as the prison siren went off. The whole shooting incident had lasted less than thirty seconds.

The driver of the canary-yellow Cadillac threw his M-16 into the unlatched trunk, followed by his pistol and the top part of his fake MP uniform. He reached into the trunk and pulled out one of the uniquely tailored suit jackets that had a shirt and tie attached in one single piece. One of their Hollywood mosque brothers who worked for the studios had made them for this special mission. It took the black man less than ten seconds to slip the suit jacket on and fasten the Velcro strips inside the jacket. He opened the Cadillac door and slipped over the seat. The keys were still in the ignition. He took a deep breath and drove away. Anyone looking inside the Cadillac would only see a very well-dressed black businessman, but if they leaned inside the car they would see his fatigue pants bloused into his boots.

The military policeman at the gate to Fort Leavenworth was closing the gate according to regulations when the prison siren went off again just as the canary-yellow Cadillac approached. The driver lowered his window and called out to the black MP, "Say, young man . . . could you let me out before you lock that?" The black businessman's voice was pleasant. "I'll be late for a very important meeting if I have to wait here."

The MP smiled and pulled open the gate just wide enough for the Cadillac to pass through. He let the three cars following the Cadillac pass also before he locked the gate until the alert was over. He didn't want anyone to think he was prejudiced.

The black driver of the Cadillac reached up and brushed the sweat off his forehead with the sleeves of the expensive suit jacket and sighed. "Fuck, was that a close call," he said to himself.

The intercom came on in the tower and the warden's voice filled the after-fight stillness. "Guard! What's going on out there?"

The tower guard pushed the switch and spoke in a very calm voice that seemed to have matured in thirty seconds. "A prisoner-escape attempt. The captain is down . . . wounded, and one of our MPs is dead. One of the assailants is dead and one has escaped. He's dressed in a military police uniform and helmet liner. He's about six foot four inches and is *big* . . . and I mean *big!*"

The warden's voice cut into the conversation. "Is he on foot or driving?"

"He left here on foot and disappeared behind a row of warehouses."

"Good job!" The warden turned off the intercom and almost instantly came back on the air. "What's the status of our prisoner?"

"Right now? He's on his face with a shotgun barrel kissing his neck."

"Good!" The intercom went dead.

The driver of the dirty canary-yellow Cadillac sat in an overstuffed chair across from a skinny man wearing a two-thousand-dollar suit. The office drapes had been pulled shut and the only illumination in the room came from the ultraviolet neon lights in the hundred-gallon terrarium. They gave a moonlight effect to the desert diorama inside the terrarium, which housed two live tarantulas.

The man wearing the expensive silk suit opened a small pet-store shipping box and removed a white mouse. He held the animal by its tail and opened the wire trapdoor on top of the terrarium. "I wonder if they know the difference between a white and a brown mouse." He tapped the side of the glass, trying to arouse the male tarantula, which was hiding under a corner of a small flat rock.

"I don't know, sir." The driver of the Cadillac was visibly nervous and swallowed before continuing. "Do you like the gift?"

"Yes . . . yes, I do . . . very much." The tone of the man's voice eased the fears resting inside the driver of the Cadillac. "But, Brother Karriem, we still have a problem . . . a very big problem now that you failed in your mission."

"Master Elijah, if you wish me to, I'll go back there and try again. . . ."

The skinny man's hand lifted up from the desk at the wrist and he moved two of his fingers from side to side. The movement was enough to cut the large man's conversation off in midsentence. "I don't think that would be a good idea. We've already lost one Death Angel in our attempt at rescuing Brother James. I don't need a second loss. The Nation must always end up winning in our fight against the devilbeasts!" A slight tightening in the minister's vocal cords was the only sign that there was a hatred contained in the Black Muslim leader. He leaned back in his leather chair and watched the female tarantula stalk the terrified white mouse. He formed a tent in front of his face with the fingers of his hands and smiled. "We need a special morale booster during tonight's leadership meeting." The room became very quiet as the two men watched the tarantula grab the mouse and inject her venom into the warm mammal's side. The mouse's legs twitched and the animal defecated on the sand. The minister's smile widened. He lifted his hand and waved for one of the men standing in the shadows to step forward. "Do we still have that white devil down in the basement?"

"Yes, Master Elijah." The man's voice was a deep bass that rumbled.

"Have him prepared for tonight's meeting." The minister returned his attention to the Cadillac driver. "Brother Karriem . . ." He paused, giving the hit man a chance to regain his fear. "I don't know if you are aware of the fact that Brother

James was the youngest Black Muslim to achieve the rank of Death Angel. He was sixteen years old."

"No . . . Master Elijah . . . I didn't know that. I knew he was special but I thought that was because of the money he had gathered from the brothers over in Vietnam—"

"What money?" Elijah interrupted. "Where did you hear such a thing?"

The Black Muslim leader glared at the man in the dark room. A shiver traversed the hit man's spine even though he couldn't see the minister's eyes in the dark.

Karriem looked down at the Afghan rug and stammered, "I—I—ah—" The muscled black man broke. He dropped down on his knees, shuffled forward around the front edge of the skinny man's desk, and grabbed hold of the Black Muslim minister's polished alligator shoe in both of his hands, lowered his head until his cheek brushed the toe. "Please! Please . . . Master . . . I know that I've failed you and the mosque brotherhood. Please forgive me . . . give me another chance!"

The guard had taken a step forward, holding his silenced 9mm pistol down at his side. The scene was almost comic and at minimum very ironic as the huge black man with four-foot-wide shoulders held the small, skinny man's foot.

The minister smiled down at the pleading member of his congregation and waved off his personal bodyguard without even looking at him. He knew that Brother Karriem had forfeited his life by touching him. He was the supreme leader of the Nation and couldn't be touched by the male members of the sect unless they were given permission. "Now . . . now there, Brother Karriem . . . anybody can make a mistake." Elijah looked over at the feeding tarantula and smiled; it *was* a very thoughtful present. "I want you to think of something *special* for our blue-eyed devil tonight . . . something very special. We are going to be bringing three more Death Angels into the Brotherhood tonight and I want it to be a very memorable meeting for them."

Karriem started sobbing and kissed the minister's shoe. "Oh thank you, Master . . . thank you for your kindness!"

"Go now and get cleaned up for the meeting. It will be held here in the mosque."

The Black Muslim leader kept his back to the door and

listened as the Death Angel Karriem and his bodyguard exited the spacious office. He leaned back in his chair and watched the tarantulas moving around the desert landscape in the terrarium diorama. He allowed his extreme anger to show on his face for the first time since he had heard that the rescue mission had failed.

The things that he had said to Brother Karriem about Mohammed James were true; James was the youngest Death Angel to have been initiated into the secret sect. James also had provided the Detroit mosque with a large amount of money from the sale of drugs in Vietnam. All in all, James deserved the support and gratitude of the Nation for his loyal service, but that wasn't the *real* reason Master Elijah had wanted Specialist Fourth Class Mohammed James liberated from the federal prison at Fort Leavenworth. The real reason was that Brother James knew too much about the Death Angel sect and about the fund-raising operations for the Detroit mosque. James was dangerous in the hands of the devilbeasts and would have to be either supported, liberated, or killed.

Master Elijah rubbed his chin and thought about his last meeting with James. He had been very impressed with James's fanatical desire to kill devilbeasts and was even more impressed when James had qualified for his Death Angel's wings before he had turned seventeen. Mohammed James had briefed him on his desire to go to Vietnam and kill devilbeasts during firefights instead of killing their yellow-skinned brothers. The idea was a good one and he had blessed it, and at the same time he had made it a policy that all the members of the Nation do everything in their power to disrupt the devilbeasts' efforts in Vietnam.

Elijah tapped the surface of his desk in a frustrated attempt to burn off some of the nervous energy inside him. He knew that another rescue attempt would be foolhardy and trying to kill James would be as dumb; he could only try to support his captured Death Angel and never make the same mistake again by bragging to an underling. James knew that there were Death Angel chapters in every one of the Nation's mosques throughout the United States and also in military units throughout the world.

A soft knock on his office door brought the minister out of his deep thoughts. "Yes?"

The door opened. "Master, it's almost time for the meeting."

"Thank you. Give me a few more minutes."

"Yes, Master." The door closed softly.

Elijah opened his top desk drawer and removed the small notepad where he had written the list of names that James had given him. Mohammed James was being shipped to Fort Bragg, North Carolina, for trial by a general court-martial, and the names on the list were the prime witnesses against him. Elijah ran his long fingernail down the column of names:

1. Salvador Garibaldi (POW with James)
2. *Spencer Barnett (POW with James)
3. Jeremiah McDonald (sergeant in Vietnam)

Elijah's finger went back to the name *Spencer Barnett* and remained there. He would start with him. James had informed a brother in prison that this Barnett devilbeast was the prime witness against him. Brother Karriem would be given a second chance.

Master Elijah pushed back his chair and stood up. He adjusted his clothes and inhaled a deep breath before walking to the door and turning the knob. He transformed into the Supreme Minister of the Nation and smiled when the bright light from the hallway struck his face. A group of very well-dressed men was waiting for him. Elijah nodded his recognition to each of them and then led the procession down the hall to a set of double doors. He paused and allowed one of his bodyguards to push open the heavy oak panels and then entered the room. A long conference table occupied most of the area and was surrounded on three sides by high-backed chairs. Sitting off to one side of the room were three men dressed in black suits and wearing very somber expressions. Master Elijah smiled and nodded at them. A dozen men sat in a row of chairs that lined the opposite wall. Brother Karriem occupied the chair closest to the main attraction.

A pair of spotlights attached to the ceiling behind the long conference table intersected at a spot exactly 257 inches from the front edge of the conference table; an inch for every year of black slavery in America.

The fourteen-year-old boy stood naked under the bright lights, his hands and feet tied tightly with leather thongs to a black-lacquered seven-foot pole. The ceremonial pole had been uniquely attached to a threaded hole in a specially designed base plate in the cement floor. A thick, clear plastic painter's ground cloth had been spread out in a five-foot circle around the pole.

Master Elijah took his seat and stared at the terrified child as he waited for his special guests to take their seats. The boy's bright blue eyes sparkled in the spotlights. Elijah smiled. He could see the terror. The boy licked his lips and tried to swallow. He had been told that if he spoke to anyone, he would be beaten. Master Elijah allowed his eyes to drift down to the boy's crotch. He could barely see any pubic hair, but that was due mostly to the child's having almost white-blond hair, which didn't show up as well as black hair against white skin.

"Thank all of you for coming to this very special meeting." Elijah spoke using his authority-filled voice. He was a master at changing his voice to reach any audience, and this group of men would respond only to absolute authority without a glimmer of human compassion in it. "Tonight we have three new members to present to a special gathering of Death Angel leaders from across the United States. . . ." Elijah moved his open hand around the table. "Minister Fiad from our Los Angeles mosque; Minister Mohammed Aheem from New York; Minister Rhain-Rheem representing our Miami brothers at the Sun Mosque; and Minister Fard . . ." Elijah did not like the idea of the man taking the name of Fard and allowed it to show in the tone of his voice and the pause, "from our newest mosque and Death Angel chapter in Atlanta."

Each of the men nodded slightly to the three men sitting together and then over at the assembled Death Angels from the Detroit mosque.

The fourteen-year-old boy tried staring past the bright lights in his eyes to see who was talking. But he could see only the three men sitting to his right side and a few of the men lining the wall to his left. A light coating of sweat covered his forehead even though he stood naked in the cool basement room.

"Allow me to introduce our newest members." Master Elijah held out his hand in the direction of the three somber pledges to the secret society. "First, there is Henry Phillips, who chose to eliminate nine male devilbeasts." Elijah blinked his eyes. "And then we have Mohammed Mombutu, whose mother has been a very active member of this mosque since Master Wali Farad founded this mosque . . . his *first* mosque here in 1931." Elijah allowed that fact to sink in to the membership in the room. It was important for all of them to remember where the Nation had been born and where the power rested. "Mohammed chose a more difficult task of exterminating five white women of the devilbeasts."

The room remained very quiet but a number of the assembled Death Angels nodded their heads in approval.

Elijah saw the nods and quickly added so that he could maintain his absolute control of the group, "*But* we have a very special new Death Angel joining us tonight . . . Red Wolf Moore. He asked for special permission to have a quota of *eight* devilbeast children instead of the usual four. . . . All of us here know that it takes more courage for a Death Angel to kill children than it does to kill the adult male blue-eyed devils, and a score of *eight* just to become a member is commendable and I am going to personally present Red Wolf a brand-new Cadillac Seville for his accomplishment! Brother Karriem from our Los Angeles mosque will take him outside after this meeting and show it to him—a yellow one that will remind you, Brother Red Wolf, of the gutless devilbeasts."

Karriem felt his stomach tighten, but he didn't dare let it show on his face that he cared if Master Elijah gave his car away.

"As a special treat tonight in honor of our guests, Red Wolf has provided us with a Polish devilbeast he found hitchhiking from Hamtramck to his freedom in California. . . . I must say that I like the devilbeasts' newfound love for running away from their families to join the *love* cults out west." Elijah's remark brought a couple of muffled laughs from those sitting around the conference table. All of them knew that the hippie movement was filling the highways with runaways and the pickings were extremely easy for Death Angels. Elijah added to his comment, "By the way, it should be noted that Red Wolf also got his quota the *hard* way. He got his spawn from hell in the northern suburbs right under the noses of the devilbeast police!" Master Elijah smiled and looked over at Brother Karriem. "That is *eight* devilbeast children for his Death Angel wings. . . . This one is a poor Polack, but Red Wolf was pressed for time and had to get something *locally.*" Elijah nodded and Karriem stood up. "Brother Karriem has some special entertainment for us tonight."

Elijah's two bodyguards checked the heavy drapes that covered the walls of the basement room that were designed to muffle even the loudest noise.

Karriem walked over to the child and gently brushed the long strands of fine blond hair out of the boy's eyes. He smiled at the terrified child and then smiled back at the assembled Death Angels, whom he couldn't see because of the bright lights shining in his eyes. Karriem reached into his back pocket and removed a razor-sharp hawk-billed linoleum knife. He reached over and tried grabbing the fourteen-year-olds scrotum, but fear and the cool basement room had drawn the child's testicles and penis up tight against his stomach. The boy tried looking down to see what the huge black man was going to do to him. He hadn't seen the fat blade of the knife yet.

Karriem dug with his fingers to find the boy's testicles.

"You're hurting me." The scared adolescent's voice was the only sound in the room.

One of the assembled Death Angels choked as he tried swallowing a laugh.

Karriem tugged on the boy's scrotum and then used the knife to slash it away from the child's body. Surprisingly, there was very little blood. The boy's veins withdrew back inside his body and the first scream rushed out of his lungs.

Brother Karriem turned around to face the bright lights and held up the adolescent's scrotum and testicles for everyone to see, then he threw them down on the plastic dropcloth.

Elijah nodded his approval. "The devilbeasts have been castrating the black man for centuries . . . now it is *our* turn!"

Karriem stepped back from the screaming child and allowed each of the assembled Death Angels who had been sitting with him against the wall to take a turn at mutilating the white teenager.

Master Elijah watched with his eyes half-closed as the boy's mouth opened and closed in silent agony. He always loved watching the victims die and he loved hearing them scream. An evil grin crossed his face as the boy died. He would make the devilbeast named Hitler look like a friend of mankind before he was through.

The only problem he had was Mohammed James, who could ruin everything if the devilbeasts got him to talk.

CHAPTER TWO

Recon Reunion

The nurse smiled as she pushed open the door to the private room. She always smiled when she saw the sparkle in the fire-blue eyes of her patient in room 131. He was special. She knew that she wasn't supposed to show any partiality to her patients, but Spencer Barnett had won her heart in one gigantic, emotional, love-filled explosion.

Spencer Barnett had been shipped directly to her ward from a prisoner-of-war camp in Laos. He had been in very bad physical condition when he first arrived at Walter Reed Army Hospital, but a month of intensive care by some of the best medical people in the business had made a dramatic improvement in the young recon soldier. The nurse smiled again when she thought about the first time she had seen him lying on the hospital bed in a horribly emaciated condition with his body covered with infected insect bites and jungle ulcers. What drew the smile from the woman was that even though his body had been tortured and broken, he wore a smile in his sleep that was caused mostly by the natural curl located at each corner of his mouth; it looked as if he was constantly smiling over a very private joke.

She pushed the door all the way open and entered the room beaming her best morning smile. Spencer lay on the white hospital sheets drenched in sweat. The curl was still there on his mouth but the deep wrinkles across his forehead told the nurse that he was in trouble. She ran over to the side of his bed and felt for a pulse. Her free hand rested on the soaked sheets. Spencer moaned and thrashed his head from side to side, sending pellets of sweat from the ends of his hair across the front of her clean uniform. She ran from the room to the nurses' station to get help. The staff had been expecting Spencer to have a malaria relapse. The virus had been detected during a blood test when he arrived at the medical center. The doctors had hoped that Spencer's body would have healed from the tortures in the prisoner-of-war camp before the malaria surfaced again. But it had come, and Corporal Barnett was fighting for his life.

He moaned again as the malaria fever attacked his body. The moan came from inside, created by the images that were scarred forever in his brain tissue.

He was dirty and naked, with his arms wrapped around his drawn-up legs and his back pressed against the bamboo bars of a low cage. She lay coiled up watching him from the opposite side of her pen. The sun slipped behind the tall trees that bordered the Montagnard village and instantly he felt the chill against his naked skin. She flicked out her tongue to test the air. She too felt the change in the temperature and slowly adjusted her coils. Spencer rested his chin on his knees and tried recalling everything Colonel Garibaldi had told him about large snakes.

The nurse returned to the room followed by a team of trauma medics. Spencer's personal psychiatrist had heard the emergency call for room 131 and was only a couple of steps behind the trauma team.

Spencer moaned again in his delirium and spoke just as the nurse reached his bedside. "Get the fuck away from me, bitch!" The nurse gasped and raised her hand to cover the shock that was expressed by her open mouth.

"He's not talking to you, Mary. He's delirious," the psychiatrist said to the nurse over her shoulder.

"Oh . . ." She felt reassured but was still worried over Spencer. He looked very ill.

The huge python started crawling next to the side of the cage toward Barnett. He held his breath.

"Oxygen!" The doctor standing over Spencer reached back for the face mask and slipped it over the lower part of the soldier's face. Spencer still held his breath. "What the hell is he doing?"

The snake tested the air again. Spencer stretched out his leg, planning on kicking her head if she got too close, and then he remembered what Colonel Garibaldi had told him about *looking* like an object that was too large for her to swallow. His foot was *bite* size for the thirty-six-foot-long reticulated python, and he drew it back again against his body and watched as she continued her slow approach. A thin rod came through the side of the cage about an inch in front of the snake's nose. Spencer took a breath.

"Good! He's breathing again!" The doctor held the oxygen mask tightly against Spencer's face as the soldier breathed rapidly. "Now he's starting to hyperventilate! This is crazy!"

"Not as crazy as what's going on inside his head." The psychiatrist spoke from the foot of Spencer's bed, where he could observe his patient and not be in the way of the medical team.

"You keep Mother Kaa away from me!" Spencer's voice rose and then lowered. "What do you want from me now, Sweet Bitch?"

The psychiatrist recognized the nickname of the female North Vietnamese lieutenant who had operated the prisoner-of-war camp that Spencer and Colonel Garibaldi had been assigned to. Spencer had refused to talk about the camp, but Colonel Garibaldi had given them a complete briefing, including the torture where she used the python.

"Where's your little turncoat today?" Spencer sneered at his hallucinated tormentor while the nurse next to his bed wiped his face with an ice-water-soaked pad. She was worried and it showed on her face. Spencer had been doing so well lately.

"James . . . Who else would I be talking about?" Spencer answered someone in his delirium. "I told you that I would *never* do that! One traitor per POW camp . . . that's all, Sweet Bitch!" Spencer groaned and arched his back on the bed as if he had just received a blow. "*Ugh!*" His body went totally limp. One of the doctors took his pulse as they hooked him up to a monitoring unit.

The nurse looked over at the psychiatrist, fear showing in her eyes. He closed his notebook and shook his head slowly. "He's exhausted and needs some fluid put back in his system." He nodded toward the IV stand and the wide strap they were tying Spencer's arm down with so that he wouldn't tear out the needle when he thrashed around on his bed. The psychiatrist smiled his reassurance. "He's going to be fine, Mary."

The fear was still in her eyes. She just couldn't lose him now that she had finally found a man she could love. Tears came with the thought, even though she knew it wouldn't look very professional, but she didn't give a damn.

The scene changed in Spencer's mind. He felt the red-hot end of a cigar against the tender foreskin of his penis. The scream coming from deep within his chest startled even the old emergency-room doctor who was working over him. Spencer tried reaching for his crotch with his tied-down hand and then changed and used his free hand to protect his groin from the hallucinatory attack. He screamed again in a high-pitched adolescent's tenor and pleaded, "Stop! Please! Stop . . . I won't do it again . . . I promise!" And then Spencer started crying like a small boy.

The psychiatrist ground his teeth together and watched the young soldier relive whatever had caused those scars that covered the insides of his thighs and the end of his penis. All the doctors had agreed that the scar tissue was too old to have been caused while he was a prisoner of war. The psychiatrist had tried a number of times to get Spencer to talk about the scars, but on each occasion the soldier had told him bluntly that it was none of his damn business. Spencer didn't realize the pressure that had been placed on the psychiatrist by the hospital commander to find out as much as they could about the young Army corporal before the President of the United States presented him with the Medal of Honor.

Spencer hadn't yet pieced together his private room and all the extra care he had been receiving during his stay. Even Garibaldi had been released from the hospital, and he had been a POW for years.

The psychiatrist knew a lot more about Spencer than the soldier realized. He had access to all the help he needed in gathering information on the boy—even from the FBI and the CIA. Spencer was a very hot property, and the President and the senior military leadership were very interested in his recovery.

The nurse couldn't take any more and left the room, followed by another of Spencer's heartrending screams. She nearly knocked down the head nurse when she shoved open the door.

"What's going on in there, Mary? My God! What are they doing to that boy?" The gray-haired colonel had never heard a grown man scream like that before and she had been around a long time."

"They're not hurting him. He's having a severe malaria relapse. Would you cover for me a little while?" The young nurse shook her head and rushed down the hall away from room 131.

"Oh . . . that dear, dear child." The head nurse entered the room to replace Mary.

Spencer lowered the top half of his body down between the two chairs and grimaced when he felt the pain as he tried to rise again. "Forty!" The word hissed out between his clenched teeth and he dropped down to the polished tile floor.

"You aren't supposed to exercise until the doctor tells you it's all right."

Spencer inhaled deeply and looked out the window. "I'll turn into a wimp and wear my hair in a ponytail before these hippie doctors let me work out."

Mary set the glass down on the table next to Spencer's bed; then walked up behind and helped him to his feet. She laid her hands on his sweaty shoulders and rubbed them in small circles. "You smell good." She kissed his back.

Spencer turned around and hugged her against his wet chest. The top inch of his hospital pajama bottoms was soaked with sweat. "I've got to take a shower."

"Would you like me to join you?" Mary teased.

"Sure . . ." Spencer started unbuttoning her uniform.

"Spencer! Stop that! Dr. Martin is coming to see you!" She

struggled with his hand. "Spencer! I'll be court-martialed for promiscuous conduct with an *enlisted* man!"

"Don't play with what you can't handle."

"Spencer! The doctor *is* coming . . . any minute now!" She felt a warm glow in all of her erogenous zones at the same time.

"Who's getting court-martialed?" The lieutenant colonel stepped into the private room.

Mary blushed and Spencer answered for her. "My nurse is afraid that she's spending too much time with me and is ignoring her other patients."

"She's too good a nurse to court-martial," the Army psychiatrist complimented the nurse. He knew that a love affair was developing between the two in spite of the age difference. Spencer was seventeen—almost eighteen, and she was a very young-looking twenty-one, graduating a year and a half ahead of her class. "But there is going to be a court-martial that you might be interested in . . ." the lieutenant colonel added.

Spencer paused in the doorway of his bathroom. "Whose?"

"Special Fourth Class Mohammed James . . . Does the name ring a bell?" The psychiatrist noticed the tendons bulge out on the hand Spencer held against the doorjamb.

"You know damn well it does." Barnett untied the drawstring of his blue-green hospital pajamas and let the loose-fitting pants drop to the floor. He used the toes on his right foot to flip the garment up to his hand. "I'm going to take a shower."

"I'll wait." The doctor's voice sounded very patient.

"It's going to be a *very* long shower."

"That's fine. Take your time." The lieutenant colonel looked over at the nurse. "Would you mind bringing me a cup of coffee on your way back with his clean pajamas?"

Mary nodded and left the room. She sensed that Spencer didn't like the psychiatrist.

Spencer took his time in the shower and brushed his teeth and shaved while he let the water run in the shower stall. He had been in the bathroom over a half hour before he opened the door with a towel wrapped around his waist. "Did the nurse bring me some clothes?"

The doctor looked up from the magazine he had been reading and nodded toward the neatly folded hospital pajamas lying on the foot of the bed. Spencer walked over and picked them up. He started pulling the towel away from his waist and then changed his mind and went back into the bathroom to change. Normally he wasn't shy, but the psychiatrist's eyes were always trying to penetrate; they were nosy eyes.

"Take your time, Spencer. This is a good article I'm reading." The psychiatrist knew how to play the game also.

Spencer looked at his reflection in the mirror and flexed his jaw muscles. He hadn't been broken yet, and some mighty powerful people had tried. He opened the door too fast and stepped out of the small bathroom. "So! What brings you around here today?"

"First, let's talk about the court-martial." The doctor looked up at Spencer over the top of his glasses, which had slipped down his nose. "What do you think about James's court-martial?"

Spencer went over and opened the window. It was getting very stuffy in the room. "Fine with me. He was a traitor."

"Well, that's what the court-martial is for . . . to see if he was a traitor."

Spencer dropped down in a chair near the window and looked out. "He *is* a traitor."

"Hmm . . ."

"What the fuck are you humming about!" The anger boiled out of Spencer.

The psychiatrist flashed an angry look at the soldier. "Try to remember that I'm a lieutenant colonel . . . okay?"

"Right, *sir*."

The medical doctor with the extra years of psychology realized that he had just screwed up with his patient. "Well, not *that* much of a lieutenant colonel."

"Make up *your* mind what you want to be . . . *sir*." Spencer grinned. "You're confusing me."

"We can't have that, can we?" The lieutenant colonel smiled. "Why don't you just call me Colonel Martin?"

"Fine with me, sir. You can call me Corporal Barnett." Spencer was tiring of the mind game the doctor was playing. "Look, I've got to take a nap."

"Sorry, Corporal Barnett, but we've still got some things to talk about."

"Like what?"

"Some things you talked about during your malaria attack last week."

"Look, Colonel Martin . . ." Spencer's voice filled with anger. "What I talk about when I'm sick, I can't help, and I can't help it if a bunch of *very* sick people sit around my bed and listen in on what I'm saying . . . that's not my fault. I don't want to be here and I don't want *you* to be here." Spencer went to the windowsill, hopped up on it, and looked out. He leaned as far out of the window as he could, holding on to the bottom of the wooden frame.

"You know it's against regulations to do that, Spencer." The psychiatrist lit a cigarette and rested his head against the back of the chair. He waited until Spencer came back into the room before continuing. "I'm not spying on you. I'm here to help you put some things back together again."

"Oh? Like what?" Spencer sighed. "I feel fine."

"General Garibaldi told us a quite a few things about what went on in your POW camp, and quite frankly we're a little worried about what it might have done to you mentally." The psychiatrist inhaled a lungful of smoke and paused.

"Mentally I'm fine."

"Let me be the judge of that." The doctor exhaled.

"Okay . . . what do you want to talk about?"

"The snake."

"The snake . . ." Spencer placed his index finger against his bottom lip and looked up at the ceiling. "The snake. Let's see . . . the snake. Oh yes . . . you mean that huge motherfucking python? The one the prison commander would use to scare the shit out of us with? *That* snake?"

The psychiatrist nodded.

"Well . . . *that* snake was very big, over *thirty* feet long." Spencer looked at the doctor to see if he believed him. "Really! Ask Colonel Garibaldi."

"He's a major general now," the psychiatrist corrected Spencer.

"I know, but he said that I can call him Colonel as long as I want to . . . it's a little thing us POWs have. You know—a mental *block* or something like that."

"General Garibaldi has confirmed that the snake was well over thirty feet long."

"I know that. I just didn't want you to think I was exaggerating." Spencer smiled.

"So tell me about the snake."

"I just told you. It was big."

"How did the NVA use the snake to torture people?"

"They put the people in the snake's cage overnight."

"That was torture?" The psychiatrist was trying to get Spencer to talk about his experience in the cage.

"You are one *dumb* motherfucking colonel!" Spencer got up and pulled open his room door. "Get out of here!"

"Sorry, Spencer . . . Corporal Barnett, but I'm calling the shots today. I'll leave when *I'm* finished talking."

Spencer slammed the door shut, sending a loud echo down the tiled hallway.

"Come back here and sit down. You're acting like a spoiled brat."

Spencer took a seat again on the window ledge and wrapped his arms around one of his legs. He rested his chin on his knee and looked down at the free people walking in one of the hospital's large parking lots.

The psychiatrist knew that Spencer wasn't going to cooperate and talk openly to him so he tried changing his tactics. "Answer my questions, Corporal."

Spencer kept staring out the window. He felt the old wall inside him begin to close its gates to the outside world. Mary had opened them for him, but this doctor was closing them again.

"Did Specialist James take part in torturing you while you were a prisoner?" The doctor's voice sounded like a tin echo.

It took Spencer so long to answer that the doctor was about ready to ask another question. "Yes."

"Did Lieutenant Van Pao beat you with a bamboo rod?"

"Yes."

"Did they bury you in a pit with a dead Montagnard child?"

The pause was longer. "Yes."

"Did Specialist James admit to you that he killed white soldiers in combat?"

"Yes."

"Did Specialist James take part in torturing you?"

"Yes." Spencer squeezed his leg and bit down on his knee.

"Does any of this bother you?"

"No."

The doctor sighed. "Spencer, please cooperate with me. I'm here to help you!"

"I thought we were going to call each other by our military ranks, sir."

"Spencer, dammit!" The doctor lost his temper. "You've got to let some of these things out. You can't live your whole life building walls around yourself!"

"I answered your questions." Spencer's voice was soft. The doctor failed to realize that when the young soldier's voice grew soft, Spencer was becoming very dangerous.

"I already knew the answers to those questions!"

"Then why did you ask them?"

"Spencer..." The doctor was taking a long shot, "where did the scars on your legs and penis come from?"

Spencer slowly lifted his head off his knee and looked at the doctor. His eyes were narrow slits. His voice was a soft whisper. "I've already told you that's none of your business."

"Do you realize that in less than a week, the President of the United States of America is going to present the Medal of Honor to you in the White House Rose Garden? There will be hundreds of press people watching and the whole Joint Chiefs of Staff!"

The expression on Spencer's face said *so what?*

"I'll tell you *so what!*" The doctor pointed his freshly lit cigarette at Spencer. "The President wants to be assured that you're not going to have a breakdown when that happens."

"There's one way to be *assured.*"

"How's that?"

"Don't give me the medal."

"You are crazy! You would turn down the Medal of Honor? Our nation's highest valor award?"

"Yep... I just did."

"You're kidding."

"No, I'm not. If that's what it takes for you and all the rest of these fucking people to leave me alone . . . it's fine with me." Spencer smiled. "You keep your medal and release me from this hospital."

"What is your problem!"

"I already told you . . . *you* for one." Spencer clenched his teeth. "Do you really think I would sit here and spill my guts out to you? Come on, Doc! How dumb do you think I am? You come on like you're my best friend . . . I can tell you anything—right? Sure . . . I *could* tell you anything and within a matter of hours it would be the talk of the whole damn hospital *and* appear in the *Enquirer* before the week is out!"

"My professional ethics won't allow that."

"Bullshit! You have to write a report, right?"

"That report is confidential."

"You, Doctor, are dumber than I thought. If the President is interested in *this* white trash from South Carolina, so is the press, and your '*confidential*' report *will be* common knowledge."

Spencer had made a good point and the psychiatrist knew it. He also knew that Spencer didn't have the slightest idea how much pressure was on the military because of the upcoming trial of Mohammed James. Civil rights groups were beginning to hear rumors of the court-martial and letters were being written by the thousands from blacks around the country to congressmen and the President, claiming scapegoating of the black soldier. There were even claims that Spencer Barnett was the traitor along with General Garibaldi. Those claims came from a prominent black minister in Detroit who had a very large following.

"Will you talk to me if I promise not to write a report?" The psychiatrist was making a last-ditch attempt to find out what was going on inside Spencer's mind.

"I'm *talking* to you right now."

"About the scars . . ."

"No."

"Spencer, I've reviewed all the reports on you since you first entered the foster-care program back in South Carolina. I have the staff reports on you for every day that you spent in the juvenile home. I *know* about your assault on the social workers and your constant fighting with the black kids in the home. You have a very *well-established* hatred for blacks!"

"So, I hate black? So what?"

"Specialist James's defense attorneys also have access to that information and they'll use it in court." The doctor was playing his aces. "And James has two of the best law firms in the country representing him. . . . God only knows where he got the money to pay them."

Spencer's eyes opened again and he smiled. "So that's what this is all about?"

"Yes." It was the doctor's turn to be honest.

"You're worried that I might screw up the trial."

"Yes."

"Well, have no fear. You can *report* back to your leaders that Corporal Spencer Barnett will not fail them! You have a pro here! I've been fucked with by the very best . . . I mean the very best motherfuckers in the *world!* And none of them have *broken* Spencer Barnett!"

"Spence . . . we all admire you. . . ."

Barnett jumped off the windowsill and pointed his finger at the psychiatrist. "Don't *you ever* call me Spence. Only my friends call me by that name! And you're not a friend! Now get out of here and go fuck with someone else's mind." Spencer was starting to breathe heavily. "You don't understand, do you? I've had a hell of a lot tougher emotional vampires try to feed off me than you! You've read their *reports*. You heard what *they* had to say, so why mess with me?"

"I want to hear *your* side of the stories."

"Oh? Well that's a bit too late, isn't it? I mean, *they won*. Did they tell you that the South Carolina juvenile system was ninety-five-percent *black*? Of course, *none* of those black boys had done a damn thing to be in the system . . . just us five percent whites. Did they tell you that some of those fine black specimens of male pride tried holding me down one night to buttfuck me? Hell no! They wrote down in the report that *I* attacked *five* seventeen-year-olds when I was fourteen! Right!" Spencer's voice began to rise. "Did the report you read state that the staff heard nothing? Nothing, that is, until one of the blacks ran over to his cage and asked for help. Yeah, I was fucking them up. This white trash has a virgin asshole and it's going to stay that way!" Spencer tapped his chest hard with his finger.

The psychiatrist was getting the reaction from Spencer that he wanted. The young soldier was finally talking.

"You don't have to worry about me making an ass out of the brass. We've solved two of your problems here today, Colonel: I've turned down your medal and I've assured you that I won't do anything stupid, like call James a nigger in court. You've had a very good day and maybe they'll skip over bird colonel and make you a brigadier general for your service to your country!"

"Don't be sarcastic."

"Sarcastic? Me?" Spencer pointed at his chest. "That's all I've ever wanted was to be left alone . . . *alone*."

"If you cooperate with me, I promise that you'll be out of here within a month."

"A *month!*"

"Or less."

"What do you want me to do?"

"Take a series of psychological tests."

"No."

"Then you'll be in here a lot longer than a month."

"I don't think so."

"What did you say?"

"I said I don't think so." Spencer went to his bed and laid down with his hands laced behind his head. He looked up at the ceiling. "I'll be out of here before the week is over."

"Really? You know that I have an awful lot to say about that." The psychiatrist ground out his cigarette butt in his coffee cup.

Spencer closed his eyes, ending the session. "You can turn your tape recorder off now, I'm done talking."

The shocked expression on the doctor's face went unnoticed by the patient. The FBI agents had assured him that the tape recorder under the loose doctor's smock would not be noticed by Barnett and it hadn't. Spencer had guessed that the doctor was wearing a tape recorder by the way the man sat in the chair and the uncomfortable way he had twisted when the machine became warm or the tape pulled against his skin.

The doctor hurried out of the room and closed the door behind him.

Spencer waited until he was sure the doctor had left and then sat up on the bed. He reached under his pillow and removed the letter he had just received from his old recon teammate. He had read the letter at least a dozen times. The familiar handwriting eased the loneliness he was feeling. If it weren't for Mary, he really would have gone crazy a long time ago. Spencer opened the letter and started reading:

> Hello, Spence!
>
> I hope you're getting better. We were beginning to worry there for a while and then we got your letter. Screwing a nurse! I'm proud of you, boy! You southern boys are really sneaky, I bet she didn't even know she had been laid until you started into your short strokes.
>
> The war is still going on. I miss having you watching my rear!

Spencer reread the last sentence. He missed being back in Vietnam with Sergeant Arnason and David Woods.

> They busted Shaw and Simpson but the VC killed both of them before the MPs could arrest them. You won't believe this shit but Simpson was buying his dope from two VC officers! No shit! Kirkpatrick got wasted. It's a long story that I'll save until we can talk face to face.
>
> They gave us some new guys on RT BAD NEWS. We lucked out and got some good men. Sanchez is a hard ass from down south and has proved himself already under fire. Warner is a rich and I mean a rich fucker from Michigan. A place called Bloomfield Hills. He's cool. I've never seen a man so good in the jungle. I mean it's *impossible* for him to get lost. We got a Polack named Koski too. I think you'd like him the best. The guy is recon all the way!
>
> Arnason made sergeant first class! How about that shit! I made buck sergeant, but it's no big deal. They

were talking about giving me my own team, but between you and me, I want to stay with Arnason until my tour is up.

We had a big fucking fight up in Khe Sanh. Mark my words, that fucking place is going to blow apart one of these days. The brass used our recon company and a company from the Marine Force Recon Battalion as a screen along the border. The NVA curled our flanks and kicked a lot of ass. It turned into a big fucking fight. I could have used you there.

The last six words of the paragraph stayed in front of Spencer's eyes: *I could have used you there*. He looked out the window and whispered to himself, "I could have used you there. Oh man, how I wished I *was* with you, Dave!" Spencer started crying. A large tear dropped down on the paper and smudged the ink. Spencer finished the letter.

Oh! Before I forget! Sergeant McDonald flew in from Nha Trang (he told me to tell you hello). I don't know what they talked about (Arnason isn't talking) but it had a lot to do with you and James. I hear he's some kind of psychopathic killer or something. I didn't like the motherfucker when he was here and I don't like him now. *You watch out for him—hear!* McDonald said that he was flying back to Washington, D.C. as a witness in James's court-martial (I know he'll look you up when he does) and Arnason might fly back with him. Who knows, they might take me along too!

I hear that you've won the Big One! Congratulations, I know you've earned it.

Well, Spence, the war calls.

Your war brother,

Sergeant David

P.S. Eat your fucking heart out, *Corporal!*

"Fucking leg, motherfucker!" Spencer spoke affectionately under his breath to a pigeon that had landed on his windowsill and was pecking at the pieces of toast Spencer had broken up and placed there for the birds. "This corporal will run circles around his sergeant ass!" The bird cocked its head, ready to fly away. Spencer looked at the bird and reached up to wipe the tears off his cheeks. "Well! Are you going to eat or just stand there fucking staring at me?" The bird pecked at a piece of toast in response to the soldier's question.

The door opened and Mary stepped in. "Are you busy?"

"A little." Spencer kept his back to her.

"Do you want me to come back?" She saw his shiny cheek and knew that he had been crying.

"Could you give me a couple of minutes alone?"

"Sure. I've got to check on a cancer case down the hall . . . a retired lieutenant general. He's not hard to deal with at all, but his wife is a bitch!" Mary went back to the door pretending that she hadn't noticed Spencer's tears. "I'll be back in about twenty minutes . . . okay?"

"That'll be fine."

The door closed behind the nurse.

The two children walked down the hallway on each side of the medium-height man. Mary looked up from her duty desk and smiled. The children were cute. The boy's hair was brushed and slicked down for the hospital visit and the girl wore her light brown hair pulled back in a ponytail. The children smiled up at the nurse when the man stopped in front of the counter.

"Excuse me, could you direct me to Spencer Barnett's room?" The man smiled, showing a set of pearl-white teeth.

Mary looked closely at the trio. She could see that they were all mixed blood and figured they were Amerasians. She was right in one of the cases, but the children were Eurasians from Vietnam. The man was from Korean stock. "I'm sorry, but Corporal Barnett is not allowed visitors, especially little ones." She saw the look of disappointment appear on the children's faces. "I'm really sorry, kids."

The man reached up and removed a folded pass from his shirt pocket and handed it to the nurse. She read the special-permission slip for the trio to visit with Spencer and smiled as she handed it back. "Signed by the hospital commander, no less! You have powerful friends."

The man shrugged and smiled. "A couple, I guess."

"I'm on my way to his room right now, let me guide you." Mary reached down and took the little girl's hand and the pair of them led the way down the corridor to room 131.

Spencer looked up from his bed where he had propped his pillows against the headboard and lay staring out the window at the fluffy white clouds that were riding a stiff breeze. Trung tugged away from Mary's hand and ran to his bed. She crawled up and hugged the familiar figure. Jean-Paul jumped up on the opposite side and wrapped his arms around Spencer's other side.

"What in the hell!" Spencer started laughing and then looked up and saw Reggie standing in the doorway with Mary.

"Surprise!" Trung's soft voice filled the room.

"What are you guys doing here?" Spencer looked over at Mary for an answer. She shrugged.

"We came to visit," Reggie answered. "Dad's in a big meeting over at the Pentagon and we decided that it was time to see you." He took a seat at the foot of the bed and watched Spencer rub his hands through the kids' hair. "Dad had to really pull some strings. They've got you locked up here in the security ward."

A shocked expression covered Spencer's face. "Security?"

"Yeah . . . didn't you know? Man, we've been trying to visit you since they put you in here." Reggie glanced over at the nurse.

"Spencer, they made me promise not to mention it to you." She looked down at the scuff marks on the waxed floor. "That's why we always used the back elevator when we left here. It was so you wouldn't see the signs posted out front."

"Why?" Spencer's voice revealed the hurt he was feeling over the deception.

"I don't know if I'm allowed to tell you."

"Why?" The anger in his voice scared the kids and Spencer immediately hugged them to reassure the preteens that he wasn't angry with them.

"They don't know what you're going to do." Mary felt very bad about taking part in the deception, but the decision to place him in the high-security ward had been made when he first arrived at the hospital. "Spencer, *all* POWs are put in here until they recover—"

"Recover? I haven't recovered?" Spencer shook his head. "Colonel Garibaldi has been out of here for weeks!"

"He cooperated with the psychiatrists. . . ." Mary's voice dropped.

Spencer laughed. "Then I'm going to rot in here or escape." He turned his attention back to the children. "You guys want to help me plan my breakout?"

"Yeah!" The ten-year-old boy sat up on the bed and crossed his legs. "We could sneak you out on one of those hospital carts. I saw that on TV last night."

"Good thinking!" Spencer laughed but his eyes flashed his hurt to the nurse.

"Spencer?" Seven-year-old Trung's voice drew everyone's attention.

"Yeah, Dove . . ."

"Why are you and Reggie always in the hospital?"

It took a couple of seconds for the question to sink in and then Reggie began laughing. He had been in the hospital in Vietnam to have his lung removed after being shot, and now the very next time they were back together again, Spencer was in a hospital bed. To the seven-year-old, the correlation was that American soldiers were always sick. "Trung, Spencer is better. He had a few bad days back in Vietnam and came here to get some medicine."

"Oh." The girl was satisfied with the answer from her adopted big brother.

"So, how are you two guys doing back here in the States?" Spencer kissed the girl's forehead. It felt good being next to the kids again.

"I like school." Jean-Paul smiled.

"He's getting straight A's!" Reggie interjected.

"Really?" Spencer ruffled the boy's hair and it fell more naturally into place.

"Yep! And I'm on a Little League baseball team!" Jean-Paul wiggled on the bed in his excitement. "I play shortstop!"

"I'm taking tap dancing!" Trung tried gaining Spencer's attention.

"Now *that's* a show at our house. Dad's about ready to

volunteer for duty back in Vietnam! *Four* girls in tap dancing and one in gymnastics!"

"I thought there were *six* girls?" Spencer knew that Reggie had five sisters before his father rescued Jean-Paul and Trung from Vietnam and adopted them.

"There *are!*" Jean-Paul's tone of voice said it all. He was outnumbered.

"Hey, sport! We hold our own now!" Reggie reached over on the bed and lifted the small ten-year-old up in the air and roughhoused with him for a couple of seconds.

"Yeah, but when you're away in college they try bossing me around all the time." Jean-Paul flashed a glance at his sister.

Mary stood in the background and watched the warm scene. She noticed how close the two children remained to Spencer and how they constantly reached over and touched him as if they were trying to pass some of their energy over to him through his skin. It was very good medicine. She saw the glow coming back into Spencer's eyes.

"We do not!" Trung spoke the words like a mother.

"Hah! You try making me play house!"

"You're always the father!"

"All right, kids . . . easy now . . . Spencer is sick, don't forget," Reggie said to calm the kids down.

"So what's your father up to here in Washington?" Spencer dropped his head back against the stacked pillows and the kids settled down again, one on each side of him.

"I don't know exactly, but I *think* he's being assigned to a general court-martial review board." Reggie looked out the window. "You've heard about James?"

"A little."

"A couple of black hit men tried busting him out of Leavenworth."

"No shit!"

"Yeah, one of them was zapped and the other one got away. The FBI is looking for him."

"Where's James now?" The question was loaded.

Reggie glanced at Spencer. "I was told that I couldn't tell you that."

"Why?" Spencer was becoming very angry.

"You got me, buddy. A lot of weird shit is going on." Reggie looked out the window again so that he didn't have to look in Spencer's eyes.

Spencer looked at Mary. "Go tell the shrink that I want to talk to him as soon as my visitors leave."

Mary hesitated and then left the room.

"It's really good seeing you again, Reg." Spencer's tone of voice changed completely when the nurse had left the room. All the facade was gone and his pain showed through.

"Are you okay?" Reggie felt the anguish in his old recon buddy.

"Yeah . . . I just need to get out of this damn place for a while." He hugged the kids tightly. "Thanks for bringing the kids with you. I need this." The children responded to the pain they saw in Spencer's eyes by snuggling even closer to him.

"Do you want me to talk to Dad?"

"Yeah, have him talk to Colonel Garibaldi too . . . maybe they can pull something off."

"You mean Major General Garibaldi?"

"Yeah."

"Consider it done."

"Thanks."

The psychiatrist entered the room and the conversation stopped. The first thing the doctor noticed was the two children curled up on each side of Spencer and the relaxed expression on his patient's face.

"Well look, we have to be going. . . ." Reggie sensed that it was time to leave.

"So soon?" Trung's soft voice pleaded with her brother.

"Yep, the doctor wants to give Spence a *shot!*"

Dr. Martin grinned. "What do I have here, *three* patients in one bed?"

Jean-Paul had had his share of shots when he was in the hospital in Vietnam from the wounds he had received from a 122mm rocket. He slipped off the bed and stood next to Reggie. Trung gave Spencer a rushed kiss and joined her brother. Jean-Paul glanced over at the doctor, decided that he would risk it, and quickly hopped back up on the bed and kissed Spencer.

"I think these kids *like* you." The psychiatrist started his mind games.

"Believe it or not, a few people actually do." Reggie had caught the tone in the doctor's voice and now leaned over and kissed Spencer's cheek. The kids giggled. "Later . . . Spence."

Spencer laced his hands behind his head and smiled at the doctor. Let him figure that one out on his own.

The doctor waited until they had left before commenting, "You have some *close* friends there."

"War buddies." Spencer winked at the doctor.

"You're a hard one to figure out." The psychiatrist sighed. He wasn't kidding. "What do you want?"

"Out of here." Spencer kept the smile on his face. "Something is going on and I've got a strong feeling that I'm a major player. My price for cooperation is getting out of here."

The doctor smiled. "That could be arranged with a little cooperation."

Spencer smiled back. He was getting very good at playing mind games.

CHAPTER THREE

Secrets

The rain added to the gloom surrounding the meeting. Stars flashed in the room from the shoulders and collars of the officers who were assembled around the oak conference table. The sergeant major of the Army looked at each of the faces and recognized most of them from prior assignments and his long Pentagon tours. He recognized newly promoted Brigadier General Jack Seacourt from one of his tours with the 82nd Airborne Division stationed at Fort Bragg, and nodded. The general nodded back but didn't smile. The assembly was too serious for friendly smiles.

"Gentlemen, please grab some coffee and take your seats." The white-haired lieutenant general spoke from the end of the table as he dropped a thick manila folder down on the polished wood.

The sergeant major set his mug on a folded piece of paper so he wouldn't mark the wood tabletop and crossed his legs to one side. He was the only enlisted man in the room and he knew that the only reason he had been invited was that Specialist Fourth Class Mohammed James had requested in writing that enlisted men be appointed to sit as members of his court-martial. This was one meeting the sergeant major really did not want to attend.

"I want to thank all of you for taking the time out of your very busy schedules to fly here on such short notice, especially Jack Seacourt, who left Vietnam early yesterday morning and has been traveling since then."

As the one-star general nodded at the lieutenant general heading the review board, everyone else in the room was staring at him. The prisoner snatch his special unit had conducted had made him famous and there was a little more than the normal jealousy from his peers.

The three-star general shifted in his seat and continued talking in a husky voice. "Gentlemen . . . I've been in the Army for thirty-four years and this is the worst thing that I've ever had to deal with." The opening remark was profound. "I know that the secrecy of this meeting has a couple of you a little baffled, but very soon you'll understand why we've taken so many elaborate precautionary measures. First I want to go around the table and introduce each of you." The senior general started with the man in civilian clothes to his right. "Mr. Manning is representing the Federal Bureau of Investigation; Mr. Templar is from the Counter Intelligence Agency; Colonel Chan is a law officer out of the JAG office." He switched to the other side of the table. "You all know the Sergeant Major of the Army. . . ." The senior NCO nodded. "Major General Koch is from the Special Forces Center at Bragg; Colonel Sinclair is a special assistant to the secretary of the Army; you've just met Jack Seacourt; and Lieutenant Colonel Tom Kemp is from the First Cavalry Division in Vietnam." The lieutenant general looked over at the JAG officer. "Have you gotten an opinion yet on Kemp?"

"Yes sir. Under the *Manual for Courts-Martial,* Lieutenant Colonel Kemp is considered far enough removed from the accused's unit to be eligible to serve on the board."

"Are you *sure?*"

"Yes sir."

"Brigadier General Heller is an instructor at the Senior Staff College and an expert on military affairs." He glanced over at the officer sitting next to the wall away from the conference table. "Dr. Martin joins us from Walter Reed Army Hospital. He's the psychiatrist who is treating our star witness, Corporal Spencer Barnett."

Colonel Sinclair and General Seacourt caught each other's eyes; both men were surprised.

"Gentlemen, you have all been called here for a briefing on the charges against a Specialist Fourth Class Mohammed James. . . . This is a very unique court-martial for a number of reasons: first, he's black . . . second, he's being charged with killing white soldiers in combat . . . third, he's aided the enemy and spied for the North Vietnamese. . . . All of these charges are *alleged*." The general looked over at the two men in civilian clothes. "And our civilian counterparts have a few charges of their own and will have the opportunity to brief us. First let's have Colonel Chan read the charges."

The Army colonel wearing Judge Advocate General Corps brass on his collars stood up and an overhead projector came on. The charges were flashed on the screen:

ARTICLE 118. MURDER.
(a) Twenty-three counts.

ARTICLE 104. AIDING THE ENEMY.
(a) Two counts.

ARTICLE 105. MISCONDUCT AS A PRISONER.
(a) Forty-seven counts for the purpose of securing favors from the enemy.
(b) Nine counts of maltreatment of fellow prisoners.

ARTICLE 106. SPIES.
(a) One count of espionage against the United States and her allies.

The colonel gave the assembled military men and civilians a chance to read the charges before he spoke. "As you can see, gentlemen, we have a major problem. Black soldiers are already complaining that they are being treated unfairly in Vietnam, and now this. We have to court-martial him, but the greatest care must be taken that the soldier's rights are not violated in any way."

"What the colonel is saying is that this case could be the spark that could shatter this country and for sure cause a major rift within the military. Gentlemen, we are talking about a soldier who is being accused of murdering his fellow soldiers in *combat* just because they happen to be *white*."

The FBI agent lifted his hand, trying to draw the general's attention.

"Yes, Mr. Manning."

"We should note here that five of those alleged murders took place in Detroit as an initiation into a Black Muslim sect called the Death Angels."

"Thank you." The general nodded at the special agent. "Sergeant Major?"

"Yes sir."

"James's attorneys requested that there be enlisted men on the general court-martial board. According to our friends in the legal office, three of the seven-man board will have to be enlisted. Can you give us a list of recommended names from preferably minority groups?"

"Yes sir. I'll have a list by close of business today." The senior NCO sipped from his coffee cup to cover his embarrassment. His eyes kept going back to the screen and the list of charges. How could any soldier betray his country and his fellow soldiers like that?

"Thank you, Sergeant Major. Also, the court-martial will be held at Fort Bragg in a secure area called Camp McCall." The general thought that now was a good time to qualify why they had chosen the isolated training camp. "Two men tried breaking James out of prison at Leavenworth last week. One of them was killed and the other escaped. We think that there will be other attempts to break him free and also possible attempts on the lives of the prime witnesses and possibly even those members serving on the court-martial board." The general looked quickly at each of the officers.

"Who are the *prime* witnesses?" General Heller asked.

"The main witnesses are Corporal Barnett and Major General Garibaldi from the Air Force, who served in the POW camp with James. There's also a Master Sergeant McDonald from the Recondo School in Nha Trang, and a Sergeant Woods who supposedly saw James dressed as an Army captain in the Twenty-fourth Corps Headquarters, and a Marine lieutenant colonel who swears that James came into the operations room and traced major battle plans." The general caught the sick expression on the face of the major general. He smiled to himself. Koch had always taken the safe way out of everything all during his Army career, ever since they had been classmates at West Point. The lieutenant general had personally selected the major general to be president of the general court-martial. Politics was a way of life for a Pentagon officer and major events such as this were a way to get rid of one's enemies and at the same time keep other enemies too busy to strike back.

"General," Colonel Sinclair spoke up from his chair, "I don't know if I'm eligible to sit on this board."

"Why is that, Reggie?"

"I know a couple of witnesses for the prosecution. Barnett and Woods. They served with my son on a recon team in Vietnam."

Lieutenant Colonel Martin became very interested in the sharp-looking Colonel Sinclair.

"I don't think just *knowing* a witness will disqualify you, but thanks for bringing it up. We *must* ensure nothing screws this case up! Colonel Chan . . . would you check this out for us please?"

"Yes sir, but I'm sure he will still be qualified as long as he's not going to appear as a witness himself."

"Let's go around the table. . . ." The lieutenant general pointed with the stem of his unlit pipe at the FBI special agent. "Mr. Manning?"

"Good morning, gentlemen. I have only a little information at the present time but I feel it's significant nonetheless. Specialist James has bragged on a number of occasions that he would never stand trial. The incident at Fort Leavenworth proves that he means what he says. The two men who made the attempt at breaking him out of the prison came very close to succeeding and I'm glad to say that a number of the prison's policies have been changed because of the attempt." The special agent looked around the room and then rested his eyes on the white-haired lieutenant general. "I have to be very careful in what I say next because we don't want to prejudice the case against James." He took a long sip from his tepid coffee before continuing. "We think that James is associated with a radical movement called the Death Angels. They are the military arm of a religious sect called the Nation of Islam. Buford Heneri is the leader of the sect and goes by the name of Muhammed Elijah. We have never been able to penetrate any of their secret meetings, but we've heard *rumors* that human sacrifices are made."

"Rumors?" Major General Koch interrupted.

"Rumors from a number of different sources." The special agent smiled. "We don't react to rumors, but we do *listen*."

"What kind of human sacrifices?" Colonel Chan asked the question now that the major general had opened up the floor.

"We think that they use the sacrifices as a bonding tool for something more sinister."

"What the hell can be *more* sinister than human sacrifices?" General Koch adjusted his seat farther back from the conference table in an effort to psychologically detach himself from the proceedings. He had maneuvered politically to gain the command of the highly prestigious Special Forces Command at Fort Bragg, but he was neither qualified nor truly interested in the men of that command. He was an Army officer and was using the position as a stepping stone to a shot at the Chief of Staff slot in Washington. The lieutenant general knew that, and that was why he had selected Koch as the president of the general court-martial board. There was a good chance that whoever held that position would lose his ass, politically.

The FBI agent looked at the major general out of the corner of his eye and then back at the senior officer, who nodded his approval for him to answer the question. "Our office in Detroit is currently investigating the mutilation and murder of a fourteen-year-old boy. Windsurfers on Lake Saint Clair found the body floating near the shoreline. It had been wrapped up in a half-dozen garbage bags and tied with a rope. Air pockets had been formed and the bundle floated just under the surface. The kids thought at first that it was a bundle of garbage, but one of them was keen enough to notice a small streak of blood leaking out of the package and waved over one of the police boats." The agent swallowed before continuing. "The boy had been hacked to death . . . his scrotum and testicles had been cut off, and I think the worst part was the look of terror that had been frozen on that kid's face. . . ."

"You saw the body?" Colonel Chan; the legal officer, asked.

"I'm assigned to the Detroit office." Mr. Manning started tapping the top of the table with the eraser end of his pencil. "There's been a rash of unsolved kidnappings in Oakland County and all of the victims have been white boys between thirteen and fifteen, all but one of them was blond with blue eyes and all of them were considered very handsome by their peers." Manning sighed. "We think this Muslim group is involved with the missing kids and we're hoping that all of them haven't been . . . haven't been murdered like the boy we found in the lake."

"What does this have to do with James?" General Koch flexed his jaws.

Manning looked over at him. "James was a member of the cult before he joined the Army and we have photographs of him with the dead man who tried breaking him out of Leavenworth. The dead man was one of these Death Angels and we're almost sure that James is one too."

"What the hell is all this talk about *Death* Angels?" Koch was becoming very nervous.

"Well, General . . . *simply* put," answered Templar, from the CIA, "we think that Death Angels are a secret organization of black males who kill whites *exclusively*. Now do you know what that means, General?" Templar's tone of voice was extremely patronizing. "That means *if* Specialist James was a member of this group, *and* they specialized in killing whites, *then* we don't just have a psychopathic murderer on our hands but *one*, I underscore the word, *one* of many organized murderers on our hands, and it is interesting to note that the Nation of Islam has chapters in every single metropolitan area in the United States and even overseas with the armed forces."

"We know that Death Angels have to kill and prove it to get their *wings*, but we don't know how many victims are needed." Manning's voice had taken on a very deep tone.

"Damn!" The single word from the psychiatrist was an appropriate ending to the special agent's briefing. He was the first one in the room to fully realize the extent and the impact.

"Thank you, Doctor." Manning nodded at the psychiatrist and ended his briefing with a closing sentence. "I hope all of you gentlemen realize how many missing kids there are every year in the United States, and this hippie movement has put thousands of kids on the highways."

Major General Koch's face turned white. He had seven sons and his fifteen-year-old had just run away. "Does this cult have one of their mosques in North Carolina?"

"I don't think so, but they have a very large one in Washington, D.C.," Manning answered.

A little color came back into Koch's face. As soon as this meeting was over he was going to call back to Fort Bragg and have them intensify their search, and then he promised himself that he was going to spend more time with his kids.

"Mr. Templar? Do you have anything to add?" The lieutenant general lit his pipe and the pleasant odor of Captain Black pipe tobacco filled the room.

"Only that we have evidence that Specialist James was seen leading North Vietnamese patrols dressed in American uniforms. The sightings were confirmed and photographed by our agents in the field." Templar looked over at Colonel Chan, who was sitting next to him.

"I pass, General." Chan shook his head as he thought. He had been assigned by the Army's Judge Advocate General to be the law officer for the general court-martial and on his shoulders rested the responsibility to ensure that a mistrial didn't happen. "But to ensure we don't cause a mistrial, I recommend that this group doesn't meet again until they're in court."

"I agree. I just wanted to let all of you know how severe the consequences can be." The lieutenant general looked over at Koch. "You're going to have a very tough task ensuring that the proceedings at Camp McCall are secure, but I don't think you'll have too much of a problem, seeing that you command a couple of thousand of the best soldiers in the world."

Major General Koch nodded.

"I hope that you're planning on using loaded weapons?"

Koch smiled a weak grin and nodded.

"Good . . . we don't want a repeat of what almost happened at Leavenworth. Don't forget—the press will be allowed in the courtroom."

Major General Koch's face went white again. He hadn't

figured that he would have to deal with the press, but James had a constitutional right to an open trial.

"We can help you out there." Manning, from the FBI, spoke up. "We've issued most of the major press corps clearances and have a pretty good idea which ones are procommunist and tend to support the radical groups."

"Thanks." Koch's voice was weak.

"Before we close this meeting . . ." the lieutenant general looked at the psychiatrist, "can you tell us anything about our prime witness?"

"Well, sir, I know you understand that almost everything that takes place between a patient and his psychiatrist is confidential—"

"I *know* that, Colonel! Is he healthy enough to take the bench at James's trail, is what I want to know!"

"Yes sir . . . he's a very tough young man."

"I hear that the President is going to present him the Medal of Honor next week." The lieutenant general's comment caught the attention of everyone in the room.

"I hope so." Lieutenant Colonel Martin let the comment slip out.

"What do you mean?"

"Corporal Barnett has refused to accept the award." Martin's voice lowered.

"He's *refused* our country's highest award?"

"Yes sir."

"That's ridiculous!" The senior officer couldn't imagine anyone turning down the most coveted award in the military. *Preposterous!*

"He has refused even to be fitted for a uniform. I've been working with him since he was released from the POW camp in Laos, and I must say he's a hardheaded young man." Martin sighed as if to emphasize his efforts at helping the troubled soldier.

"Well, we can't allow him to refuse the award!" The lieutenant general hit the conference table with his fist. "Do you know what that will do to this court-martial? How will it look? Our prime witness refusing his country's highest award! The defense will tear us apart!"

The psychiatrist nodded in agreement with the general and then shrugged and added, "I can try talking to him again, sir."

"Try! You *will* convince him." The lieutenant general huffed and then added, "What in the hell do you psychiatrists *do?*"

Colonel Sinclair smiled and cut in. "General, if you don't mind . . . I might be able to help."

"How?" The senior officer was angry.

"I might be able to persuade this young man to accept the award."

The lieutenant general looked at Sinclair through the cloud of pipe smoke that divided them, then he looked back at the psychiatrist. He saw the worry creep into the medical man's eyes over the suggestion. "Fine . . . I'll have a pass waiting for you at the main desk at Walter Reed. When can you go see him?"

"Right after this meeting?"

"Excellent!" the lieutenant general agreed.

"Sir! I don't think that's a very good idea. A stranger visiting Corporal Barnett might upset him too much and give him a relapse." The psychiatrist was worried. He wanted to have at least a couple of hours with Barnett before the colonel talked with him.

"Bullshit! Colonel Sinclair isn't going to send the boy back to a POW camp! Personally . . . " The general pointed at the psychiatrist with the chewed end of his pipe stem, "I think you damn shrinks do more *damage* to a person than good!"

The psychiatrist's face turned red.

The senior general sensed that he had hit his target and added, "You stay away from this corporal until Colonel Sinclair has talked with him."

"Sir! I'm a medical psychiatrist! You can't order me away from my patient!" Martin's professional honor was at stake.

"No . . . but I am the president of the colonel's promotion board that goes in session tomorrow. . . ."

Lieutenant Colonel Martin lowered his eyes to the floor. He wasn't going to screw up his chances for early promotion over *one* soldier. What he failed to realize was that the general had already made up his mind.

"All right, gentlemen, you all know what you have to do.

Let's make sure it's done right." The lieutenant general stood up, signaling that the meeting was over. "*But*, before we go . . ."

The men in the room stopped moving around and looked at the general.

"I know it *looks* bad for Specialist James. There is a lot of evidence against him and the charges are numerous . . . *but*, he is still a soldier in the United States Army and a citizen of this great country . . . He will be given all the rights due him. *Am I understood?"*

Every man in the room nodded in agreement.

Colonel Sinclair left his car in the front parking lot of the huge hospital complex and entered through the double doors. He began doubting himself just about the time he felt the air-conditioned breeze rush past him. He wanted to turn around and follow the cool air back outside but caught himself. He had opened his big mouth in front of the generals and now he was obligated to at least try to talk to the young soldier. He had never met Corporal Barnett, but his son had spoken often about him and Woods.

The pass was waiting for him at the main desk, with the room number for Barnett written in the left-hand corner. Sinclair took the center corridor. The halls were crowded with doctors and patients. The Vietnam War had brought a lot of wounded to the medical center and the surgeons were some of the best in the world.

Colonel Sinclair paused at the nurses' station in the wing Barnett was in and noticed that all the signs stated that the area was a security zone. Cyclone gates separated the wing from the rest of the hospital.

"Excuse me, nurse . . . could you direct me to room 131?"

A pretty, young nurse looked up from her chart and smiled. "First closed door on your right."

"Thanks." Colonel Sinclair walked briskly down the hall. The creases in his pressed khakis snapped against the tops of his spit-shined shoes. He took a deep breath, knocked on the closed door, then entered after hearing a muffled "Come in."

He didn't really know what to expect when he entered the

room, but what confronted him caught him completely off guard.

Spencer had placed two chairs in front of the window; he lay across them, with his pajama bottoms rolled up as high on his legs as he could. He lay with his hands folded behind his head in the direct rays of the bright sunlight coming through the window. The young soldier didn't open his eyes.

"Yes?"

Colonel Sinclair took a couple of seconds to study the soldier before answering. Spencer was well tanned and the colonel could see that the young man was recovering well from his POW experience, at least physically. A few blue-red scars showed up on his side and across his stomach, but the soldier's muscle mass was returning.

Spencer turned his head in the direction of the colonel but kept his eyes closed. "Can I help you? I'm getting some rays right now, and as you can see, it doesn't last very long before the buildings block it out again."

"I've come to draw some blood samples."

"Fuck! Again!" Spencer shifted his position on the hard chairs.

"Sorry." Sinclair smiled. He didn't know why he had said that to the soldier.

"How much?"

"A couple of quarts."

"What!" Spencer sat up and looked over at the smiling officer. "Who are you?"

"A friend."

Immediately a suspicious look filled Spencer's eyes. "Of who?"

"Actually, I'm a friend of some of your friends."

"That fucking psychiatrist *isn't* a friend of mine."

Colonel Sinclair tilted his head slightly to one side. He found Barnett's comment interesting. "Why? Don't you like your doctor?"

"Not really. Are you a shrink?"

"Hardly . . . I'm an infantry officer."

"I can handle that. . . . I'm recon out of the First Cav." Spencer's voice carried his pride in his unit.

"I know."

The question appeared through Spencer's eyes.

Colonel Sinclair saw the flicker of mischievous light in Spencer's eyes and agreed with his son partially: Spencer did look like a cocky bantam rooster, but the gleam in the young soldier's eye reminded the old warrior more of a mischievous elf. Spencer was small framed but layered with a strong set of muscles. The young man's real strength, though, was *inside* the layer of skin, deep inside.

"My son was on your recon team."

A light broke through Spencer's eyes and the blue brightened as he read the colonel's nametag. "Reggie?"

Sinclair nodded.

"He was just here with the kids!" The natural curl at the corners of his mouth enlarged as he smiled. "Why didn't you tell me right away who you were? I thought you were one of those damn head doctors . . . man, am I sick of them."

"Why are you being kept in here?" Colonel Sinclair looked around the room and asked a blunt question: "Are you violent?"

"I can be."

Sinclair glanced up and saw the mischievous smile again. "You like to jack people around, don't you?"

"Some people more than others."

"I like you." The honest, open comment caught Spencer unprepared to answer. Sinclair walked over to the open window and reached up to gently shake the Cyclone screen. "This place would *drive* me nuts."

"Me too." Spencer hopped up onto his bed and dangled his feet over the edge. "It was sure good seeing Jean-Paul and Trung again. It was nice of you to take them in."

"Not really . . ."

Spencer stared at the colonel, trying to figure out what he meant.

"They've brought more to my family than they've taken from us . . . much more."

Spencer blinked. "Now I know why Reggie and Woods talked so much about you in Vietnam."

"Yeah . . . I met Woods when I was visiting Reggie in the hospital. He was a really impressive soldier."

Spencer smiled. "Woods is a pussy!"

"He sure likes you."

"He's queer."

Sinclair laughed at the intimating comment. He knew exactly what Spencer was trying to do.

"I don't know what for. You don't seem to be good-looking enough to attract that kind of person."

Spencer knew that the colonel wasn't going to fall for his game.

"Woods was really worried about you back there. He felt that it was his fault that you were captured."

"He's overprotective."

"He's a damn good friend."

"I know that!" Spencer snapped.

"Well, you're going to let him down and Reggie too."

"I'll never let my recon buddies down . . . never!" Spencer stood up and faced the colonel.

"How do you think they're going to feel if one of their *own* teammates turns down a Medal of Honor?"

"So *that's* why you're here!"

Colonel Sinclair nodded and stared directly into Spencer's eyes.

"Well, go back and tell that fucking shrink that it isn't going to work!" Spencer turned his back on the colonel to hide the tears. He was starting to break and he knew it. That bastard was using his friends and their families to get to him.

"Lieutenant Colonel Martin isn't the one who sent me here. . . . In fact, he was very upset when I told him that I was coming."

Spencer spun around to check the colonel's eyes to see if he was lying.

"I'm not lying to you, Spence." The colonel used the name that his son used when referring to Barnett.

The young soldier stared at the colonel and searched his face for any sign that the officer was in league with the psychiatrist. Spencer's lower lip quivered.

"It's all right, Spence. . . ." Colonel Sinclair held out his arms and the seventeen-year-old warrior who had stood up to horrible NVA torture, juvenile homes, and abuse from stepparents took a step forward and let the dam break.

Colonel Sinclair held the soldier and felt his own heart

ache. Spencer cried quietly but the old warrior could feel him shaking. The tears were soaking through his khaki shirt but the colonel didn't care. What was taking place in the hospital room was something that should have happened a long time ago, but Spencer needed to be near someone he trusted before he could allow that to happen. Reggie Sinclair's dad was that kind of person. He understood and didn't judge.

A knock on the door interrupted the emotional scene.

"Give us a couple of minutes!" Colonel Sinclair yelled through the closed door and received a muffled reply.

Spencer went into the bathroom and washed his face while the colonel blotted his shirt with a clean napkin. Spencer stepped out of the bathroom holding a towel. "I screwed up your shirt. Fuck . . . crying like a baby . . . I must be really fucked up."

"There's *nothing* wrong with you, Spence. . . . Don't tell anyone, but I cried in Korea . . . in Vietnam . . . and in fact, I just cried last week when they buried a good friend of mine in Arlington." Sinclair smiled. "Warriors cry too."

Spencer tried grinning. "Yeah . . . it did make me feel a little better."

"Watch out, though—too much crying will make you queer." It was the colonel's turn to grin.

"Shit!" Spencer fell back into his old role. "This here white trash from South Carolina has had too much pussy to turn back now!"

"Right! You and Reggie both!"

"I can't speak for your son." Spencer smiled a wide, honest smile. The tears had washed away a lot of his pain.

"What can I do for you, Spence?"

"Can you get me *out* of here?"

"Where do you want to go?"

"Sir, this place is driving me nuts!" Spencer's voice lowered. "Anywhere . . . just a couple of weeks . . . maybe up in the Blue Ridge Mountains. I know a nurse here who might let me use her family's summer home."

"Call her in here." Colonel Sinclair knew that he was sticking his neck out, but he also knew that if Spencer broke, a great deal would be lost, and that included the young soldier himself.

Colonel Sinclair waited in the stuffed chair while Spencer ran out the door and over to the nurses' station. He returned a couple of minutes later pulling the same cute nurse Sinclair had seen when he arrived.

"Sir . . . this is Mary." Spencer almost stuttered in his excitement.

"Mary?" Sinclair smiled. "Enlisted men now call lieutenants by their *first* names?"

Spencer and Mary blushed. "Come on, sir . . . give us a break."

"This *one* time." Colonel Sinclair kept smiling. "I can see why Spence likes you." She blushed even more. "Spence tells me that you have a place in the mountains that he might be able to use for a couple of weeks."

"Yes, we have a place up in the Shenandoah Valley, but—"

"But what?" Sinclair had already guessed what was coming next.

"But . . . we've made a rule that when someone is up there a member of the family has to be there also. I have a couple of weeks' leave coming to me." Mary smiled shyly at Spencer.

"Sounds like a bribe to me." Sinclair kept smiling.

"It is." Mary touched Spencer's hand.

"Let me make a couple of telephone calls." Colonel Sinclair turned to leave. "Would you give me the address, please?"

"Sure. Let me walk you out to the desk and I'll get a pad and pen." Mary squeezed Spencer's hand and let go.

"Spence, pack up your things. I'm going to try to get you released from here today."

"Today?"

"Within the hour, I hope."

"Colonel."

Sinclair paused in the doorway.

"You're right about the medal. If I don't take it, guys like Billy-Bob, Lee San Ko, Kirkpatrick, and Clancy Brown will never be remembered. I owe it to my team."

Sinclair nodded in agreement. "As long as you live and have a mouth, they'll never be forgotten."

Spencer nodded and turned to look out the window. He felt

like crying again, but that would be *too* much. Once in a lifetime was enough for white trash out of South Carolina.

Mary looked up from the note she had written for the colonel with the address of their summer home on it. "Colonel, I don't know why you're doing this for Spencer, but it's the best thing that could happen to him right now. Thank you."

Colonel Sinclair smiled. "No thanks necessary. Spencer Barnett doesn't know it, but he saved my son's life."

CHAPTER FOUR

Montagnards

Heat seemed to radiate off everything in the jungle in the form of steam. The rain had just stopped and as soon as the clouds disappeared the tropical sun beat down on the wet vegetation.

Sergeant Woods stopped and turned around to face back down the trail. He was acting as the recon team's rear guard. He listened for a good minute and then moved on. Warner was acting as the point man. The Bloomfield Hills, Michigan, soldier's mother would literally have had a heart attack if she had known that her son was performing such dangerous duty and especially on a reconnaissance team. She thought he was serving in Saigon under a general officer whose family lived near their Georgetown townhouse in Washington, D.C.

Sergeant Arnason clicked his tongue and the patrol came to an instant halt. Only Woods moved along the trail until he caught up to the team, and then he stopped. Arnason listened to the jungle. The whole team knew that they were in Laos, a neutral country, and their capture or exposure would embarrass the United States government, especially since President Nixon had told the whole world that there were no American troops in Cambodia or Laos.

Arnason signaled with his hand for the team to circle around him. Woods slipped next to the team leader and waited until Warner had joined them off the point. Koski, the big Polish man, kept his back to the team and watched the jungle to the north, while Sanchez watched to the south. RT BAD NEWS was the best recon team in the First Cavalry Division and their reputation was legendary. The black-dyed Marine fatigue caps they wore brought free drinks in any bar in I Corps, and that included free drinks from Marines and Navy types alike. Once, a couple of Marines tried taking the caps away from the Army team and a riot nearly broke out until a Marine who recognized the silver skulls on the caps pulled the other Marines aside and whispered into their ears. A series of apologies followed, along with a half-dozen drinks. RT Bad News had bailed out a couple of Marine Force Recon Teams from a very bad situation along the border a couple of months earlier and a great deal of respect was held for that team.

Arnason leaned over and whispered to Warner, "How close do you think we are to the rendezvous site?"

Warner didn't hesitate and pointed a little to the left of the trail. "Two hundred meters."

Arnason nodded. "Good . . . Everyone be on the lookout for an ambush." He looked over at the single Montagnard who had accompanied the team as an interpreter. "Are you all right?"

The small Vietnamese Indian smiled. He was in his element.

"Good. Let's move out. . . . David, cover our rear; Koski, stick close with that M-60."

The big Pole nodded.

Warner took the lead again and started moving through the jungle. He had been following the natural contour of the hill along an overgrown deer path and veered slightly to his left. Warner needed to look at a map only *once* of a small area such as a ten-square-click recon zone and he recalled everything in his head. Once he was oriented on the ground, it was impossible for him to get lost, day or night. He was phenomenal.

The jungle opened in front of Warner almost instantly. One second he was struggling through a thick patch of finger-sized bamboo and the next instant he was standing in a man-made clearing. He took a quick step backward and lowered his weapon. The clearing was empty. Arnason moved forward and joined Warner. The point man indicated that this was the rendezvous site. Arnason scanned the edge of the fifty-meter-wide clearing and saw nothing, yet he hesitated on stepping out in the open. He tapped Warner's shoulder and then Koski's and pointed to his left. He wanted them to circle the small clearing to the left, while he would take the right side with Sanchez and the Montagnard. Woods would remain there and act as a covering force and a point of reference in case they made contact with the NVA.

A small man stepped away from the jungle on the far side of the clearing. He carried a folding-stock AK-49 and an NVA canvas chest pack with six extra magazines. A machete hung from a cloth belt around his waist. He wore the traditional costume of the Bru. The Montagnard interpreter noticed immediately that the man was authentic Bru and wore the color-coded vest jacket of a Bru chieftain. The man they had come all the way from the A Shau Special Forces camp to meet was standing fifty meters away.

"Him here." The interpreter whispered in Arnason's ear and pointed.

Sergeant Arnason hesitated and then stepped clear of the jungle. He was still not sure if this was an NVA trap, using the Montagnard chief as bait.

The short, barefoot man started walking across the clearing toward the American and Arnason followed suit and walked out to meet him, carrying his CAR-15 slung over his shoulder. The interpreter followed close behind. He was from the Sedang tribe north of Kontum, but he could easily converse with the Bru.

The interpreter was the first one to break the silence with a common greeting. The chief gave a curt nod and asked for proof of their association with the blond American.

Arnason looked around the clearing and saw that the edge of the open circle came alive with Montagnard warriors. Some of the camouflaged little men had been only a couple of meters away from his teammates and had not been seen. Arnason was impressed. He reached into his jacket pocket and removed a plastic bag that had been neatly folded and slipped the photograph out so the chief could see it. There were five men in the photograph, two on each side of Spencer Barnett.

The chief recognized the young blond soldier and smiled. He looked at Arnason a couple of times and then back down at the color photo before he tapped it and grunted.

"He accepts the proof." The interpreter's face showed his relief. He wasn't going to worry the Americans unnecessarily, but if the chief hadn't accepted the photograph as proof of their friendship with the Amerian soldier who had been a POW in his village of A Rum, they would have all been killed on the spot.

Sergeant Arnason remained looking at the Montagnard chief but spoke to his interpreter. "Ask him if it is safe to remain here."

The interpreter spoke and the chief looked around the area and then spoke to his men.

"We go to their village for the night. He said for your men to walk with him." The interpreter smiled. They were being honored. "Don't fear. You will be safe with the Bru. The American, Spencer Barnett, is honored by these people."

Arnason nodded and waved for his team to join him in the clearing. He took a deep breath as he directed his men to walk close together behind him and the Bru chieftain. The team sergeant knew that they would be safe with the Montagnards, but all of his training and experience in the jungle was being rubbed the wrong way.

The walk to the hidden Bru village followed the natural contours of the ground, and even though the trail went through some of the densest jungle in Laos, the walk was easier than a normal recon patrol. Warner watched carefully and learned a great deal from the Montagnard scouts. He realized that they had doubled back a number of times on the trail to remain along the natural ridges of the steep jungle-covered hills. The walk was longer but much less tiring than humping over the hills and ridgelines the way Americans traveled through the jungle. The column of Bru stopped and Warner tried looking over the heads of the men in front of him to see what was going on. The column started moving forward again, but this time much slower until it was Warner's turn to drop down and crawl on his hands and knees through what looked like a pig tunnel through a very thick patch of bamboo. The Montagnard who stood next to the tunnel touched his index finger to his lips in the international sign to keep quiet. The tunnel turned a couple of times in the fifteen-foot crawl and then opened up on a very wide trail. Warner could see the pig tunnel on the other side of the NVA trail and realized the Montagnards had made the "pig trails" to camouflage their trail that intersected the enemy path.

The village was more compact than normal in the triple-canopy jungle, but the Montagnard renegades had to hide not only from the NVA soldiers but from American observer aircraft. The Bru didn't trust anyone outside their village and were surviving in a very hostile environment because of it. A near hit by an arc-light bombing mission had forced the Bru chief to make contact with a couple of CIA operatives in Laos and he asked for protection from the American blanket bombings. The CIA had been hoping the renegade chief would make contact with them and they could work together against the NVA, but the chief trusted no one outside his village.

The reason for Arnason's liaison with the chief was based on Major General Garibaldi's debriefing to the Army intelligence and the CIA people back in Washington, D.C., and it was working. Garibaldi had read intelligence reports back in the Pentagon that told about a group of renegade Montagnards who were causing all kinds of havoc with the NVA forces in that region of Laos where his old POW camp had been. Garibaldi had worked with the CIA and had designed this plan using Spencer Barnett as the focal point. He knew the old Bru chief liked Spencer a great deal, and through the young soldier they had hoped to make liaison with the Bru and be able to supply and direct them against the North Vietnamese.

Sergeant Arnason was impressed with the village and noticed the lack of domestic animals, which made sense. Pigs and cattle would make too much noise and draw the NVA to the village. The chief led the Americans to the guest longhouse and spoke to the interpreter.

"The chief says for you and your men to stay in the longhouse for the night as his guests. It is a great honor." The interpreter smiled. "He says that when it becomes dark"—the small man pointed to the edge of the cliff they were standing near and drew a line with his hand to show that when the shadow from the cliff reached the opposite side of the narrow crevice was what the chief had meant by becoming dark—"you come to a *num-pah* ceremony."

Arnason smiled and nodded at the chief.

Koski waited until they had entered the guesthouse before asking his question: "What's *num-pah?*"

"Rice wine that is newly fermented, and it gets you *very* drunk." Arnason dropped his backpack down on one of the woven bamboo mats that the Montagnards used for beds.

"We going to get drunk?" Warner's voice reflected his concern. "Out here in the jungle?"

"I hope *only* me. If they offer you guys the wine, try and fake your way through it. I know that I won't be able to with everyone watching, and getting drunk is considered honorable." Arnason shook his head. "I don't mind getting drunk . . . it's the hangover the next morning that kills me."

"You're our *leader.*" Sanchez dropped his pack down on the mat at the far end of the longhouse, near the exit. "It looks like you'll have to show us how it's done."

"Fuck you, Sanchez!" Arnason dropped down and rested his head against his pack. "I suggest we all get some rest while we can."

"Can we trust these Yards?" Warner's voice sounded nervous.

"As much as any ally . . . besides, we're in their village and really don't have much of a choice anymore." Arnason looked around the hooch. "Where's the interpreter?"

"He stayed outside with the chief. The last I saw of him was when they entered the longhouse." Koski nodded toward the other side of the compound."

"Maybe we'd better keep a guard posted—just in case." Arnason crossed his legs and pulled his black Marine fatigue cap down over his eyes. The silver skull had been covered with a piece of green cloth tape.

"I'm not tired." Koski carried his M-60 in the crook of his arm like anyone else would carry his hunting rifle. He had a hundred rounds of ammunition in the pouch hooked to the side of the light machine gun. The big Pole stepped out onto the platform porch attached to the entrance to the hooch and sat down cross-legged to watch the activity in the village. He noticed right away their interpreter talking to a very old Montagnard on the porch of the longhouse across from them. The old man kept pointing toward him and the interpreter would nod and make a long speech about something. The whole scene made Koski nervous, especially since he couldn't understand what they were saying.

Three hours passed before the interpreter left the old man and hurried across the narrow clearing to where Koski sat with his back against the wall of the guesthouse. Koski hadn't bothered waking up his reliefs.

"Where is the sergeant?"

Koski nodded toward the entrance. The interpreter went inside to wake up Arnason while Koski remained outside watching the Montagnards moving around the longhouses. Everything seemed very normal, with children playing quietly near the buildings. Koski could hear Arnason talking to the Montagnard inside the hooch.

"I have learned many things from the old chief. He tell me about the white-haired boy the NVA kept in a cage in A Rum."

"Spencer Barnett?"

"I am sure that is who he talks about. Old chief says that the white-haired boy was very brave. Boy argued with NVA when NVA want to kill his grandson. Boy tell NVA that he will take the grandson's place on the bamboo stake!" The interpreter was very impressed. "That a very brave thing to do, and all the Bru now talk about the white-haired American boy! You show old chief's son the magic picture of you and white-haired boy smiling together and now the old chief wishes to help you fight the NVA. He say they kill many, many NVA and put them on stakes like they did to his grandson."

"Stakes?" Arnason didn't understand what the interpreter was trying to say.

"Yes. Take and cut off bamboo still growing in ground." The small man used his hands to show Arnason what he was talking about; at the same time, his facial expressions showed the pain a person must feel when they were tied and then shoved down on the sharp stakes through their rectums.

"The NVA did that to a small boy?" Arnason felt his stomach roll.

Woods had been listening with his cap still pulled down over his eyes and his head resting against his pack. The interpreter was answering a couple of questions he had had ever since they'd rescued Barnett and the Air Force colonel from the POW camp.

"NVA kill small boy . . ." the interpreter held up nine of his fingers to show the boy's age, "with the stake and make whole Bru village watch. Spencer Barnett yell at NVA officer that he will take boy's place on the stake and the NVA laugh and say . . . okay. They play with white-haired American soldier and only lift him up and let his"—he pointed to his rear end—"touch the end of sharp stake and then they place Spencer Barnett in front of stake. . . ." He showed with his hands a distance of about three and a half feet. David Woods lifted the corner of his cap so that he could see. "NVA kill chief's grandson and leave boy on stake for three days . . . in sun." The interpreter wrinkled his nose, trying to show the horrible smell of the decomposing body. "NVA leave American soldier to watch . . . three days." He lowered his head. "Then NVA make American soldier, Spencer Barnett, dig hole to bury boy. . . . Boy's father watched from jungle . . . and NVA make American soldier fill hole this much"—he showed about a foot of dirt with his hands—"and make Spencer Barnett sit on top of dead boy, and NVA bury Spencer Barnett in dirt. . . ." He drew a line with his finger across his neck.

David Woods closed his eyes under his cap. He had seen a small hand in the dirt under Spencer when they had dug him out of the hole where the NVA had buried him up to his neck. Now Woods knew who had owned the tiny hand and why Spencer was so screwed up mentally when he was rescued. It must have been horrible for Spencer to have to sit three feet away from a little kid and watch the flies and bugs crawl over his body and then crawl over his own. Woods squeezed his eyes together hard. He fought back the tears.

"Fuck . . ." Arnason whispered the word with more expression than a whole speech would have made.

"Chief you meet in clearing is the dead boy's father. He declare the Bru enemies of the NVA. All dead NVA are placed on sharp stakes in jungle to tell other NVA that the Bru are at war with them."

Arnason nodded. The small band of renegade Bru were causing the NVA to hold back over a division of infantry to guard and reinforce the trails and supply depots in Laos. The NVA wanted the Bru dead and would give anything to find their secret villages in the jungle.

The small interpreter leaned over and looked out the open doorway. "It is time to join the Bru warriors for the *num-pah*."

Arnason got up on his feet. "Let's go, Woods, Sanchez . . . Warner." The men struggled to their feet, trying to work the knots out of their tired muscles at the same time as they were slipping on their gear. They took everything with them but their backpacks. "Sanchez, bring one of your claymores with you . . . and the hand detonator."

Arnason led the way across the clearing to where the Bru chiefs and some of their senior warriors waited. The dark shadows had filled the narrow valley and it looked almost as if night had fallen already. The interpreter took a seat next to Arnason and spoke a greeting to the Bru chieftains for the Americans. It was very important that no one was offended during the ceremony.

Sergeant Arnason noticed the American dog tag hanging from the old chief's neck almost as soon as he got within sight of the chief. He controlled his curiosity until the interpreter had made all the proper introductions and then Arnason asked the chief where he had found the small metal tag.

"One of his warriors found it sticking in the side of a cliff near a tiger's den." The interpreter nodded over at the old chief's son who was wearing a beautiful necklace that was made from a set of huge tiger claws.

Arnason spoke to the Sedang interpreter. "Ask the chief if I could look at the steel tag, because it has a name on it and I would like to know if it belonged to one of my missing men."

The interpreter spoke and the old chief smiled and removed the dog tag. He handed the leather thong and tag to Arnason, who nodded and smiled as he took it. The tag was shiny from being worn around the chief's neck and the stamped name and identification was easy to read:

FILLMORE
BILLY-BOB

Arnason's eyes slipped over his ex-teammate's social security number and blood type and rested on his religion:

PENTECOSTAL

"Fillmore's . . ." Arnason spoke to Woods. "I guess we can report back that he's dead."

"We could," Woods shifted his position and slid closer to Arnason to whisper, "but he comes from a dirt-poor family down South. They'll draw his missing-in-action pay until someone *confirms* his death. We haven't *seen* any body or bones."

"You're right. Let the rich motherfuckers *pay* at least. Seeing's the poor folk are fighting the war for them." Arnason was bitter.

Warner ignored the comment. He agreed with the sergeant, even though he was from an extremely wealthy family; he was a rare case in Vietnam.

"The chief would like for you to drink first." The Sedang interpreter held the long bamboo straw over to the sergeant. There was no way to cheat when drinking from the huge ten-gallon community bowl because a piece of bamboo had been laid across the open top of the jar and a spur from the bamboo had been bent down into the milky liquid. Each person drank from his straw until the tip of the bamboo spur was out of the rice wine, and then the jug was filled to the top again and another person drank using his straw. At any given time there were a dozen straws in the jug at once, but only one person drinking at a time.

Arnason finished drinking and sucked in a deep breath of air. "Whew!"

The Montagnards laughed and slapped their bare legs. The Americans were funny. The chief nodded in approval of Arnason's prowess and drank from his straw.

Sergeant Arnason waited until all the men sitting around the clay jug had taken a turn drinking the rice wine before removing his treasured custom-made Randall survival knife from his ammunition belt. He took his time removing the blackened blade from its leather sheath. The Montagnard warriors sitting around the wine jug were impressed when Arnason showed them how sharp the blade was by shaving some hair off the back of his forearm, but when he removed the cap from the handle of the knife and removed the matches and fishing line complete with hooks, the chief's eyes lit up.

Arnason slipped the blade back into its sheath and handed it to the old man. He spoke to his interpreter. "Tell the chief that the knife was made by a man in my country who is famous for making knives. Tell him also that the knife can be turned into a spear by putting a bamboo shaft in the handle."

The interpreter spoke rapidly to the chief and poked with his hands as if he were using a spear. The old man laughed and nodded.

"He is very pleased with your gift."

The Sedang Montagnard nodded in approval and added, "Montagnard people like knives."

David Woods saw the look of envy in the young chief's eyes and did one of the smartest things he could have done. He removed his Randall knife off his web gear and handed it to the young chief. The knives were both survival models, except Woods's knife had a stainless steel blade.

The young chief grinned, showing all his stained teeth, and spoke rapidly to one of his warriors, who then disappeared into one of the longhouses.

Arnason lifted the claymore up in the air so that everyone sitting on the porch could see it. "Ask the chief if his warriors know how to use this."

"He say yes. Many of his people have been soldiers with the CIDG camps in Vietnam."

"Good. We've brought nine of them with us that he can have." Arnason nodded. A claymore ambush in the jungle was a deadly thing.

"Chief say for you to drink more *num-pah*."

Arnason nodded and leaned over to take his straw. He saw a bug floating on top of the white liquid and started drinking. He could feel a buzz start in the back of his head and was thankful that he had thought ahead and taken a handful of pills that included aspirin and no-shit tablets.

The Montagnard warrior returned carrying a small handwoven cloth in both hands. He took a seat next to the young chief and waited until the leader reached over and took the package. All the warriors drank from the jar before the young chief whispered to his father and the old man raised his hand for everyone to be quiet. Many of the villagers had been watching the drinking party from the shadows.

"What's going on?" Arnason's voice was becoming thick.

"Shit . . . you've got me." Sanchez was already drunk.

"Man . . . this wine goes right to your head." Warner was feeling the effects worse than Sanchez.

The chief started talking rapidly in Montagnard and kept patting the cloth package. He spoke for a good five minutes and then opened the top of the cloth and removed a thick metal bracelet. He held it in the air for everyone to see, and all the Montagnards gasped in awe, including the Sedang interpreter. The old chief presented the bracelet to Sergeant Arnason.

"Thank you, Chief." Arnason nodded and smiled.

The young chief removed another bracelet from the cloth and presented it to David Woods, who thanked him and blushed.

The interpreter remained silent. He was shocked over what had just occurred. The young chief removed three more bracelets from the cloth and presented the rest of the team with Bru friendship bracelets.

The wine flowed until way past midnight. Arnason and all of his team, with the exception of Koski, were very drunk. The Montagnards had not been offended by Koski's refusal to drink; they realized that a war was going on and some of the warriors had to be able to fight in case of a surprise attack.

Koski started carrying the Americans back to the longhouse in the bright moonlight that filtered through the overhanging trees. He didn't waste time putting them inside but dropped each of them on the porch. As soon as Warner closed his eyes he threw up. Sanchez heard Warner and threw up next to him over the edge of the raised platform. It was good that they were so drunk they didn't see the village dogs eating their vomit.

It was the hot rays from the morning sun that finally forced Arnason to roll over and groan.

"You should be getting up, Sergeant." Koski's voice sounded like cannons in Arnason's ears.

"Oh . . . ugh!" Arnason tried swallowing but the stomach acids from his vomit had burned his throat.

"There's a stream nearby where you can wash up." Koski helped Arnason to his feet.

"*Never* again . . . ever!" Arnason forced out the words. "I don't give a fuck if it insults the whole Asian nation!"

Koski glanced over and saw Woods blink. "Let's go. Time to get your sorry asses moving!" Warner rolled over onto his side and then quickly crab-walked to the edge of the porch to gag.

Koski supported Arnason as they walked across the open area between the longhouses. Some of the villagers looked up, but most of them ignored the drunk Americans. They all knew that *num-pah* was very powerful stuff. Koski lowered Arnason next to the narrow stream and turned to go back and get another of his teammates. Woods and Sanchez were staggering across the clearing. Koski stepped aside and let them pass. He grinned and was very glad that he had not taken part in the rice wine. Warner was lying flat on his back when Koski returned to the porch.

"Let's go, party boy." Koski chuckled. "Don't they teach people in Bloomfield Hills how to drink?"

"Fuck you, Koski! You Hamtramck Polacks are given beer in your baby bottles!" Warner tried opening his eyes and groaned. "Oh . . . I'm going to fucking die . . . am I fucking drunk!"

"Come on, the cold water down in the stream will do you good."

"Koski, I can't fucking move. . . . I mean it. If I move, I'll *die!*"

Koski reached over and grabbed Warner's arm. He pulled him across the porch until he could get a good grip on him and then threw him over his shoulder.

"Oh! Please!"

"Shut up!" Koski carried Warner gently to the stream and set him down. Arnason had removed all his clothes and was stretched out on his back in the shallow water. Woods and Sanchez were splashing water on their heads. Warner looked at his teammates and then staggered out into the center of the waterway and sat down. The ice-cold mountain stream felt so good that Warner lay back in it and let the fast-moving water rush around his throbbing head.

Koski returned to the longhouse and gathered the team's gear together on the porch. He looked around for the Sedang interpreter and saw him exit one of the communal houses where he had spent the night with one of the younger girls. Koski carried the team's weapons and web gear down to the stream. Arnason was getting dressed and Sanchez and Woods had joined Warner in the center of the cold stream. A group of Montagnard boys had gathered on the bank and watched as the crazy Americans tried sobering up.

"How are you feeling, Sarge?" Koski asked Arnason.

"Better . . . but I still don't think I'm alive."

"That's a nice bracelet you got last night." Koski pointed to Arnason's wrist.

"You got one too, didn't you?"

"Sure, but mine is made out of brass. . . . Yours is gold."

Arnason lifted his arm and looked at the intricately carved pencil-thick gold bracelet. "Holy . . . ! I didn't even notice last night!" Arnason turned the band on his arm and admired the chain of elephants, tigers, and monkeys that encircled the gold friendship band.

"Woods got a gold one too. I think they're very special." Koski nodded over at Woods, who was still too drunk to notice the gold band on his wrist.

"It is a great honor to have a Bru armband made from yellow metal." The interpreter had joined them by the stream. "All Bru people will protect you and you will never go without food and protection in the jungle."

"Why Woods and me?"

"You gave the chiefs some very good gifts and their honor was at stake. Actually, it was one of the smartest moves that you could make with them. They were very scared about bringing Americans into their village."

Arnason's thoughts went to the time and he looked down at his watch. "We have three and a half hours to set up a drop zone." Arnason changed the subject from the gold bracelets to the task at hand. "Have the Bru selected a site for the air drop?"

"Yes. Chief's son will take us there when you are ready." The Sedang interpreter pointed back to the chief's longhouse, where the young chief waited in the shade of his porch.

"Is he sober already?"

The interpreter shrugged. It didn't matter if he was sober, as long as he could take them to the selected site for the air drop of weapons and ammunition.

"Let's get our stuff together. We've got to move out in an hour!" Arnason yelled at his teammates in the water.

Code words had been prearranged back at the First Cavalry Division Headquarters for the air drops, and the bundles of weapons, ammunition, medical supplies, and canned foods had all been rigged before the recon team had left the base area. All that was needed was for Arnason to signal the forward air controller and give the grid coordinates for the drop zone and the time.

Pain ripped along the base of Warner's skull with every step he took. It was extremely difficult to concentrate on the trail. He reached into his jacket pocket and removed the vial that contained powerful pain pills that were supposed to be taken only in the event of serious gunshot wounds and they couldn't be airlifted quickly by medevac. Warner figured the pain in his head was as bad as any gunshot could be and took two of the pills. Woods saw Warner take the pills and held out his hand. Anything was better than suffering from the rice-wine hangover, even getting shot.

The Montagnard guides stopped walking a couple of hours after noon and spoke to the interpreter.

Arnason waited in the shade of a large wild banana tree while the Montagnards discussed where the drop should take place. The interpreter joined Arnason after a couple of minutes.

"Bru say there is an old sweet-potato field on the other side of this mountain that would be very good for airplanes to see."

"You don't sound too happy with that idea." Arnason detected a slight hesitation in the Yard's voice.

"NVA sometimes watch the field for American helicopters that leave American soldiers jump out and then fly away."

Arnason figured he was referring to special recon teams of Special Forces men. "Do they think there are NVA watching the potato field now?"

"Yes. There are two NVA soldiers watching from a corner of the field and they have a . . ." The interpreter held his hand to his ear.

"Radio?" Arnason guessed.

"No."

"Telephone?"

"Yes!" The Sedang interpreter smiled.

"Do the Bru know exactly where the NVA are?"

The interpreter nodded.

"Good. Show me . . ." Arnason tapped Woods's shoulder and nodded for him to come with him. "The rest of you stay here and wait for us to come back."

"Where are you going?" Warner whispered.

"To check out the drop zone." Arnason pointed at a thick grove of young mahogany trees. "Wait there for us."

One of the Bru warriors guided Arnason and Woods to the far side of the large sweet-potato field that was overgrown with elephant grass and clumps of sweet potatoes growing wild. The sound of wild pigs rooting in the field echoed across the open ground to the Americans. The Bru warrior paused and then pointed to a dark corner of the field that was surrounded by thick jungle. Arnason guessed that was where the NVA had their observation post. He nodded and pointed, indicating that he wanted to go there. The Bru warrior grinned and started moving slowly in that direction around the edge of the field. Pig runs were cut from the jungle to the field every few meters, and for the better part of the way the three of them could use the narrow paths to walk on and not have to break through the thick bamboo and grass surrounding the field.

It took them over two hours to circumvent the field, and they nearly stepped out into the open before the Montagnard grabbed Arnason and stopped him. A soft sound of a hammock creaking caught Woods's ear and he lowered himself to the ground. The roof of an old longhouse stuck up above the tall grass. The NVA scouts were using the old abandoned Montagnard village as their observation site. Arnason wished that he had kept his knife until after the mission was over. He had to rely on his silenced .22 caliber pistol. Woods removed his pistol from its holster. The Montagnards had said that there were two men on guard.

Arnason started moving forward slowly and the Yard stopped him again and pointed to his right. The Bru was obviously familiar with the old village. He took the lead and skirted around the buildings so that they approached the last longhouse next to the jungle from a line in the shadows of the tall jungle trees.

Woods heard the NVA snoring before he saw him sleeping in the hammock. The second NVA soldier couldn't be seen. Arnason and Woods waited and listened.

A voice came from inside the hooch. The repetition of the same phrase told Arnason that the second NVA was talking to someone over the telephone and there was a bad connection.

Wood slipped the safety off his pistol and covered the sleeping NVA in the hammock while Arnason went around the hooch and located a window with the bamboo mat shutter propped open by a bamboo pole. Arnason didn't hesitate when he saw the back of the NVA soldier's head through the window. He fired. The small .22 caliber round penetrated the back of the soldier's head. The telephone dropped to the floor.

The NVA in the hammock raised his head and looked into the dark doorway of the hooch. He spoke and waited for a response. A jungle bird called to its mate, filling the silence. The soldier reached over for his SKS rifle and dropped his feet to the ground out of his hammock. Woods's pistol hissed and the NVA soldier dropped back in the hammock, dead.

Arnason stepped around the side of the building and up onto the porch. "Keep a lookout for any other gooks. . . ." He slipped through the doorway into the dark room. The NVA telephone operator lay slumped over his makeshift desk. Cooking utensils hung from pegs in the bamboo support poles along the wall. Arnason noticed that there were only two bedrolls on the floor and one AK-47 leaning next to the desk. He was sure that there had been only two guards.

"It's clear outside," Woods whispered from the doorway.

Arnason held his finger to his lips and pointed at the telephone receiver dangling from its cord. He stepped back out into the light and walked a couple of meters away from the building before talking. "Let's get back and call in the air drop. I don't know how much time we have before they send someone out here to check the guards or fix the telephone line."

Woods nodded.

The Montagnard party waited around the perimeter of the sweet-potato field, camouflaged perfectly by the jungle. A small group of Bru warriors covered the trail that led to the old village from the NVA base area farther west. It had taken only an hour to assemble the Bru for the air drop and the flight time from the American base was less than thirty minutes. The sound of the small FAC aircraft passed over the potato field and banked to the south where the L-19 pilot flew in a racetrack pattern and guided in the large C-130 aircraft for the air drop.

Woods watched the large pallets hit the ground in the tall grass of the potato field. A small herd of wild pigs squealed and raced off for cover in the jungle.

Koski was the first one out on the field and hacked through the nylon retainer straps with his machete. The pallets had been assembled with a dozen man-sized loads on each one. The riggers were good at what they did. Koski handed a pack to each of the Bru warriors, and it took only a couple of seconds for one of the Americans to make minor adjustments on each of the backpack straps before the warriors disappeared into the jungle with the supplies.

Arnason was impressed with the efficiency of the Bru warriors. It had taken them less than twenty minutes to clear the drop zone of the supplies and hide the parachutes in the jungle.

The crack of a rifle alerted the team that the Bru guarding the trail from the NVA base area had made contact with an enemy force. Within seconds the jungle erupted with small-arms fire and RPG rounds exploding against trees. The Bru fought the NVA only long enough to give the DZ party time to escape, and then they melted away in the jungle. The NVA commander found his trail watchers dead and he had nothing to show for his efforts.

The Bru moved fast through the jungle. Warner noticed that they were taking trails around the hidden village and heading toward a mass of rocks that jutted up from the jungle floor over a thousand meters into the air. The rocks were laced with caves that were almost impossible to locate unless you had a division of men and months to search.

The Bru chieftain was waiting just inside a cave entrance for Arnason and his recon team. He used the interpreter to thank them for the supplies and then he told the Sedang that the Americans would have to go back to South Vietnam. The rest of the caves were secret and the Bru would not risk showing them to any outsiders.

Arnason understood. He smiled and waved goodbye to the Bru chief. He was glad that he could move his team out of the area now that the NVA had been alerted and were starting to search the jungle. If they stayed in the caves for another day, they would be trapped there for at least a couple of weeks until the area cooled off.

Warner looked at the map and Arnason shot a direction with his compass. They both agreed on their location and Warner took a couple of minutes to orient himself before taking the point for the recon team. They would have to move fast. Right before they left, a pair of Bru warriors approached the interpreter and told him that they would guide the team to the border. The Bru realized even more than the Americans did that speed was very important if the Americans were going to escape the closing NVA circle around the area.

The small recon team moved quickly through the jungle. Too fast for Woods and Arnason, but they figured the Bru warriors knew where they were going and he was sure that the old chief wouldn't let their guides move so fast unless the trail was safe and protected by Bru scouts. They came to the edge of the river that divided Laos from South Vietnam before nightfall and thanked their guides before they left. It would be a short wait until it was dark enough to cross the river and make it to the abandoned fire-support base that was their pickup site.

Arnason leaned back against his pack and spun the Montagnard bracelet around his wrist. He figured there had to be at least three ounces of pure gold in the band, but the artwork was fantastic, especially for the Montagnards, who were a practical people and didn't waste time on detailed carvings.

Woods slipped over next to the team leader and smiled. He pointed at his bracelet and nodded. Arnason frowned and leaned forward so Woods could whisper in his ear. "Good trade . . . huh?"

Arnason smiled and agreed with his assistant team leader. It has been a very good mission and the knife for the gold band was a good trade. Just how good a deal it was would be proved in the months to come.

Captain Youngbloode sat on the hood of his jeep and watched the helicopter grow in the sky as it flew in from the west. He wore a very worried expression on his face. He was quite happy that the whole team had made it back safely from the high-risk mission, but it was the briefing he had received from the division's intelligence officers and the CIA agent that caused the deep furrows across his brow. He had never met Specialist Mohammed James, but he had read the reports and was disgusted with the man's conduct. James had set the American black soldier back a hundred years with his conduct, and Youngbloode had agreed that if what James was suspected of doing got out to the line troops in Vietnam, there would be rioting and the outcome of the war would be in severe jeopardy.

Youngbloode pressed his lips tightly together. He was angry. Guys like James screwed it up every time and had done so since the Civil War. The Youngbloodes were a proud black family and had done their share in America, but now it was time to move on, back to the old country, and rebuild from there.

The chopper touched down on the pad. Arnason could see the grim expression on his company commander's face and instantly became worried. The captain usually was smiling when a team came back from the field in one piece. Something was bothering him.

Woods waited until they had cleared the helicopter before talking to Arnason. "What's wrong with the captain?"

"I don't know." Arnason's voice reflected his worry. "I hope it isn't something we've done." Arnason's thoughts were on their recent mission. He was hoping that the NVA hadn't found the Bru village and wiped it out.

Arnason saluted the captain and smiled. "It's nice to be back, sir."

Youngbloode nodded and returned the salute. "I'm glad it went so well."

"Perfect! The Bru have the supplies and they made the whole team Bru tribesmen!" Arnason added, "Thanks to Spencer Barnett."

Youngbloode nodded. "Speaking of Corporal Barnett . . ."

Woods's face turned white and he looked over at Arnason, who instantly became worried.

"Nothing's wrong with him?" Arnason asked.

"No . . . no, he's doing fine." Youngbloode took a deep breath and looked his sergeant directly in the eyes. "It's James . . . they're going to court-martial him."

"I expected as much," Arnason stated.

"Back at Fort Bragg . . ." Youngbloode forced a smile. "You and Sergeant Woods are being called back as witnesses."

"Us?" Arnason was shocked. "Going back to the States?" It had been years since he had been back to the States.

"Yes . . . you'll be leaving this afternoon by Lear jet to Saigon and then by special aircraft to California," Youngbloode explained. "They'll brief you on the way down to Saigon. Right now, get your gear turned in to the supply room."

"I can't go. . . . What about the rest of my team?" Arnason was groping for an excuse to stay in Vietnam.

"They're being sent to Australia on R and R for a week . . . courtesy of the CIA." Youngbloode glanced over at the three men.

Sanchez slapped Warner's shoulder. "Yeah!"

"Shower and change uniforms . . . you have an hour." Youngbloode slid onto the front seat of his jeep and waved for his driver to leave. "That's an order, Sergeant!"

"Yes sir." Arnason's shoulders drooped. He didn't want to go back to the States. He had been in Vietnam over four years straight and had sworn that he wouldn't leave until the war was over.

"Come on, Sarge! It's not that bad back there in the land of the big PX!" Woods tried cheering up his team leader.

"*Shut up, Woods*!" Arnason broke away from his number-two man. *"Just shut the fuck up!"* He started running toward the fighting bunker that RT Bad News used for a team hooch.

"What's that all about?" Warner asked, shrugging.

"It's a long story." Woods watched his leader run across the open red-dust clearing and disappear into the black opening.

War had a way of fucking up a man's mind.

CHAPTER FIVE

A Gathering of Warriors

He sat on the top railing of the old split-rail fence and watched the red-tailed hawk disappear into the meadow carpeted with Queen Anne's lace and islands of yellow and orange hawkweed. The bird of prey lifted up off the ground after hopping a half-dozen steps. A young first-litter rabbit hung from one of the bird's talons and kicked its hind legs in a futile attempt to free itself from the death grip.

Spencer Barnett watched the bloody, early morning scene with a tinge of sadness. Death seemed to haunt the earth; something always had to die to make room for something new. The thought bothered him. He inhaled a deep lungful of moist mountain air and smelled the sweet scent of honeysuckle from a nearby vine. A thick mist rolled over the meadow from its hiding place in the Christmas-tree forest that bordered the south slope of the meadow. The large stand of pine and blue spruce had been planted over fifty years earlier by one of the original settlers in the valley and had grown wild.

Mary walked down the double-rutted jeep trail holding a steaming mug of coffee in each hand. She saw Spencer perched on the fence and changed her course.

"I'm glad I found you before the coffee got cold." She handed him a mug and joined him on the fence. "See anything this morning worth talking about?" She smiled around the lip of her mug.

"Flowers . . ." Spencer skipped over the hawk incident and the thoughts it had caused in his mind.

"You do know a lot about wild flowers." Mary reached down with her free hand and plucked a stalk containing bright blue flower heads that were just beginning to open in the early morning light. "What's this called?"

"Chicory . . . Do you know that each flower only lasts one day and then it dies. The roots can be dried and used as a coffee substitute."

Mary gave Spencer a teasing look out of the corner of her eye and plucked another nearby flower from its stalk. "And this?"

Spencer grinned. "Poison ivy."

Mary dropped the bright orange flower and gasped.

"I'm just kidding—that's butterfly weed. The pioneers called it 'pleurisy root' because the Indians said it cured pulmonary ailments."

Mary looked down at the beautiful flower with more interest. Her nurse's curiosity made her slip off the railing and pick up the orange flower for a closer inspection. "Really? That's interesting. . . . Where did you learn all this stuff about wild flowers?"

A long silence filled the morning air. The heavy dew made the moment seem even longer before Spencer answered her. "When I was in the foster care system down in South Carolina, one of my foster fathers taught me. The family lived on a farm."

"*One* of your foster fathers?"

"Yeah . . . the social workers believed in moving us around so we wouldn't become too attached to a family."

"That doesn't make sense."

The look Spencer flashed at her told Mary that he agreed with her statement but there was a lot more to the story. "I know it doesn't, but what makes sense to us doesn't necessary make sense to a children's welfare system that draws money from the state for *each* child in the system."

"In other words—the social workers don't want a kid to get out of the system once they're in it?"

"Bingo! Girl, you're smart!" Spencer was being sarcastic. "I call them emotional vampires . . . real vampires drink your blood, but these creatures *feed* off the emotions of others . . . probably because they don't have any of their own."

"What's this?" Mary used another wild flower to change the subject. She could tell that Spencer was becoming upset.

He glanced at the golden orange trumpet-shaped flower. "It's a touch-me-not."

Mary giggled. "A what?"

"Touch-me-not." Spencer slipped down off the fence and walked over to the low growth. "Actually, this should be growing closer to water. . . . Watch . . ." He gently shook the plant and a soft popping sound filled the air.

"What's happening?" Mary slipped off the fence and stood next to Spencer in the waist-high tangle of wild flowers and weeds.

"The seed pods explode when a strong wind shakes the plant or when an animal brushes past it." Spencer looked at Mary out of the corner of his eye.

She casually slipped her hand up over the back pocket of his worn Levi's and under his denim jacket. Spencer wasn't wearing a shirt. She set her coffee cup on top of a fence post and wrapped her arms around his waist from behind. Spencer stopped shaking the plant. With her fingernail she traced along the hair of his trail-to-paradise and stopped when she reached the waistband of his Levi's to draw tiny circles against his stomach.

"That's dangerous. . . ." Spencer's voice was husky.

"You said that *animals* make the seed pods explode when they brush a touch-me-not. Well . . . I'm a touch-me-often. . . . Make me explode."

Spencer turned around to face her and saw the look in her eyes. He used his boots to flatten a spot in the meadow and slipped his jacket off for her to lie on. Mary rubbed her hand against the growing bulge in Spencer's Levi's and pulled him down on top of her. The smell of wild flowers and the soft hum of the bees provided the extras for their early morning lovemaking.

The FBI agent dropped his binoculars and looked at his partner. "I think that kid is a billygoat."

"Again?" The other FBI agent chuckled.

"Yeah . . . again." The agent using the binoculars shook his head. "Well, I don't give a damn what the chief said—I'm not going to sit up here and watch those kids screw."

"It's your decision, but you know the rules—they're not to be out of our *sight*."

"They're not! We both know where they're at!"

The agent shrugged and kept the grin on his face. It was almost funny how often the kid and the nurse had sex. The jungles of Vietnam must have really built up a reserve in the boy.

Mary lay in Spencer's arms and looked up at the white clouds floating by. "Spencer Barnett, it gets better every time we do it."

"Thanks." He tickled her left nipple with his dry lips.

"Oh!" She feebly tried rolling away from him but the touch felt too good.

Spencer stopped and rolled over onto his back. He could feel the cool dew-covered grass against his back. Mary cuddled closer to him and shivered. "You cold?"

"No . . ." She sighed and nuzzled his chest with the tip of her nose. "I love you, Spencer Barnett."

"Me or my *Great* White?"

Mary chuckled. Her warm breath slipped across his chest and tickled. "Both of you . . . but I wouldn't call it the *Great* White."

"Oh?" Spencer shifted his position on the ground. "What *would* you call him?"

Mary waited until she knew Spencer was becoming irritated before answering him. "Oh, I'd call him . . . the *most* spectacular gigantic lady-pleaser that ever was attached to a man."

"That'll do." Spencer shrugged. "But let's call him the Great White for short."

Mary dropped her hand and felt Spencer's Great White. He was resting. "Are you done?"

"For now."

"Are you trying to tell me that that's it?" Mary teased.

"Sure . . . unless you want to do it again with that *huge* spider watching us." Spencer pointed to the large black-and yellow Argiope spider in the center of her two-foot-wide web, which was only inches away from their feet.

"Agh!" Mary jumped up and stepped back away from the spiderweb. She shivered. "Oh, Spencer! Was that there all the time?"

"Yep."

"*Oh!* Why didn't you tell me?"

"She doesn't care. I was more worried about bothering her than her bothering us."

"Let's go." Mary turned to walk back to the jeep trail.

"Aren't you going to get dressed first?" Spencer started laughing. Mary's blouse was off and her jeans were unbuttoned.

"Yes!" She started reaching down for her blouse and shivered again. "You pick it up, please . . . and shake it out."

Spencer smiled and reached down for the blouse. "Women!"

"And lead the way back to the trail!" Mary exaggerated her directive.

"If it wasn't for that patch of fur . . ."

"Well . . . that's something *you* can't change!"

Spencer stepped out onto the jeep trail and turned to take Mary in his arms. They hugged for a couple of minutes. "That's something I have no desire to change, young lady."

"Good." She kissed him. "But could you do something about those spiders in the meadow?"

"Like what?" Spencer took her hand and started walking back toward the cabin.

"Spray them or something . . ."

Spencer started laughing and Mary tried hitting him with her blouse, which she was still carrying in her hand.

The FBI agent kept the binoculars up to his eyes. "It must be nice to be a kid again."

"What are they doing?" His partner leaned the 306 against a nearby tree, making sure the scope didn't bang against the trunk.

"Walking back toward the cabin on the jeep trail." The agent shook his head and then stopped. The movement was making him sick, looking through the glasses. "She's not wearing a blouse or a bra."

"Let me see!" The rifleman reached for the binos.

"Absolutely not! J. Edgar Hoover would throw you out of the Agency if he heard you say that!"

"You're looking!"

"Yeah, but I'm on *duty.*" The FBI agent lowered his binos for a second and glanced over at his partner. "Besides . . . I've a *daughter* that old."

"Fine, tell that to our supervisor . . . but if that young soldier down there ever finds out that we've been watching him through binoculars . . ."

"I can guess what he'll do. I understand he's going to the White House next week to receive a Medal of Honor." The agent swept the meadow with the binoculars as he talked. He was a professional and knew what he was looking for as he paused in each of the shadows the trees made along the edge of the forest. The information they had received was that a secret sect was going to assassinate Spencer Barnett and the other key witnesses to the James court-martial before the court convened at Fort Bragg, North Carolina.

Spencer paused when they reached the last turn in the trail. "You'd better slip on your blouse before we reach the cabin. I wouldn't want those FBI agents checking out my woman."

Mary shook her blouse and checked the sleeves for spiders before slipping it on. She shuddered involuntarily and reached for Spencer's hand.

"I love you, Mary."

She looked up at him and smiled. "I love you too, Spencer Barnett."

"I don't think I could handle it if something bad happened to you."

"What makes you say that, Spencer Barnett?" She loved the sound of his full name and always referred to him in private as Spencer Barnett.

The two of them made the last turn in the trail and looked up at the back deck of the large mountain cabin. Mary's father had built the new log structure only the year before and had torn down the old cottage that overlooked the private lake. He had done an excellent job and the whole effect was nothing less than spectacular. A private raised wooden deck went from the master bedroom through a small stand of spruce and sweet-smelling easter red cedar out to a screened gazebo that was built overhanging the shoreline of the lake. He had built it especially for his wife, who loved to sit near the water late at night. She had died before she had a chance to use it, and now only Mary would go out there to be close to her mother.

"We have visitors." Mary saw the men on the back deck and pointed. Spencer had been lost in one of his personal thoughts—a growing fear that he would fall too much in love with Mary and then lose her.

"What did you say?"

"Visitors . . . on the back deck."

Spencer squinted and stared at the small figures standing in the shadows of the cabin. He raised his hand to his forehead, trying to block out the bright sun breaking over the tops of the trees to the east. "Are you expecting anybody?"

"No. Daddy leased the cabin to the CIA for the summer." Mary eased closer to Spencer. "Maybe they brought in some more FBI agents."

"Might be . . . some of them are wearing dark caps." Spencer squinted harder but couldn't make out much more until they got closer to the cabin. "Come on. We'll find out soon enough. . . . I'm not liking this at all!" He was becoming angry. "We were supposed to have some privacy!"

"Take it easy, Spencer Barnett! Let's find out what they want first." Mary had to take a few running steps to keep up with Spencer's brisk pace. "Slow down, Spencer Barnett, or I'll never talk to you again!"

Spencer caught himself and waited for her to catch up. He noticed that two of the figures on the porch were facing his direction and leaning against the back railing. One of them was wearing a dark cap and the other stood ramrod straight.

The closer they got to the deck, the faster Spencer walked until he was nearly dragging Mary by her arm. When he saw the light flash off the silver skulls on the black Marine fatigue caps, he knew for sure who was on the deck.

"Mary! It's Sergeant Arnason. . . ." He recognized the soldier standing next to Sergeant Arnason and cried, "And . . . and David Woods!" Spencer let go of Mary's hand and ran to the steps leading up to the deck. He was greeted by a pair of wide smiles.

"Going for a morning walk or *pretending* that you're still a recon man?" Arnason broke the emotional deadlock.

"Arnason!" Spencer raced over and grabbed his hand. "What a surprise!"

"Yeah . . . we figured we'd better stop in and check you out before you got into a lot of trouble back here." Arnason waved his open hand across the deck. "*This* is a hospital?"

Spencer grinned and hugged his teammate. "Dave . . . man, is it good seeing you!"

"Believe me, the feeling is mutual. We just got off a mission in Laos. . . ." Woods glanced at the woman standing alone at the head of the stairs.

Spencer looked back over his shoulder and his face turned red with embarrassment. "Mary . . . I'm sorry!"

"That's okay . . . introduce me." A slight edge of jealousy was in her voice. She didn't like sharing Spencer with anyone and it was obvious that these men meant a lot to him.

"This is my team sergeant, Dwight Arnason . . . and my best friend from Vietnam, *Sergeant* David Woods."

Woods cut in, "Very good, Spence, you remembered—*sergeant* . . . that's me."

Spencer hooded his eyes and grinned. "Bite my ass . . . Sergeant!"

"And who's this" Mary looked over at the master sergeant who stood quietly in the shadows.

Spencer noticed him for the first time and his breath caught in his throat. "Sergeant McDonald?"

"Yeah, boy. That's me." The NCO stepped out from the shadows and she saw the green beret on his head.

"What are you doing here?" Spencer was shocked.

"James's trial . . . I'm a witness." The older man walked over to the railing and the light reflected off his face from the sun coming up over the roof.

Mary's breath stuck in her throat. She couldn't believe how much the sergeant and Spencer looked alike . . . almost like father and son.

Spencer held out his hand as if he was going to shake and then changed his mind and hugged the soldier. "Man, have I missed you. I didn't even have a chance to thank you!"

"For what?" the burly Green Beret sergeant said over Spencer's shoulder as he hugged the young man.

Arnason winked. He knew how much McDonald meant to

Spencer, and so did Woods. The man was Barnett's father figure, and both of them had figured out that it was a mutual feeling.

"For busting my ass loose from that POW camp!" Spencer hugged harder.

"You're making me jealous, Spencer Barnett!" Mary came to the rescue.

McDonald smiled. "I need a drink after all that hugging shit!"

"Through the French doors and on your left." Mary pointed to the deck doors that led to the den and bar area.

"Thanks." McDonald entered the den. He needed the break. The whole scene was becoming too emotional. No one knew how much Spencer looked like his son who had been killed in a car wreck when he was only thirteen. That had been his initial attraction to Spencer and it had grown. McDonald saw the oak bar and poured himself a half-glass of booze from one of the cut-crystal decanters. He hoped he had selected bourbon by the color of the liquid, but it turned out to be a very good brandy. He drank it anyway and looked back outside through the large-paned windows at Arnason and Spencer talking. The young soldier's mouth was curled at the edges in a constant smile that forced anyone talking to him to smile back.

Mary entered the den through the French doors. "I see you've found it."

"Yes, thank you. It's a bit early for drinking, but I've had a long trip and my system is still operating on Vietnam time."

"No problem." She nodded back over her shoulder. "They are really close, aren't they?"

McDonald sensed the jealousy. "War has a way of bringing men together . . . *close*."

"I know . . . but it makes me jealous."

"You're honest." McDonald held up his glass and toasted the nurse," Cheers! That's rare nowadays."

"I love him . . . Sergeant McDonald."

"If we're going to be friends, how about calling me Jeremiah or Jerry."

"I like Jeremiah—it's a powerful name."

"I can see that you're very special to Spencer. He needs a woman who he can love right now in his life."

"Right *now?*" Mary's voice turned cold. "What about later?"

"Spencer's the kind of person who loves *totally.* He wouldn't ever recover if you left him once he loved you."

"I know."

"How?"

"Just by the way he acted on the deck. When he saw you standing back by the steps and he realized he had left you for his friends, he looked like a man who left his house to go to work without his pants on."

Mary threw back her head and laughed. If only the sergeant knew how close they had come to catching Spencer without his pants on. "I guess you're right. A man needs male friends too."

"Good ones." McDonald sipped the brandy and then held the glass up to the light. "Good stuff."

The door opened and Spencer stuck his head inside. "What's going on in here? I heard laughing!"

"You'd better keep a better eye on this young lady, boy, or you're going to lose her!" McDonald finished his drink and set down the glass. "I've got to go unpack. The Agency is putting us up here for a couple of days."

"Great!" Spencer was genuinely happy.

"Spence!" Woods called from outside.

"Mary, I'll be on the deck for a while if you don't mind."

"Sure! Have a good time until lunch!" Mary winked at McDonald. He was right: she had nothing to fear from his war buddies. No one would take Spencer Barnett away from her.

Woods stood near the redwood railing holding his hand behind his back.

"Whatcha got?" Spencer smiled.

"Guess." Woods held out his free hand to keep Spencer away from him.

"Don't fuck with me! Whatcha got?"

Woods brought his hand out from hiding and Spencer's eyes clouded. "We thought you might still want this. . . ."

Spencer took the black-dyed Marine fatigue cap and turned it around so that he could read the tag sewn across the front above the silver skull: RT BAD NEWS.

"Naw . . . I don't wear shit like this anymore." Spencer pretended that he was going to toss the cap over the railing and then started laughing. "I love it!" He slipped it onto his head. "Where did you find it?"

"When we went back to search for you after the . . ." Woods felt the emotion building up again and skipped over the capture of Barnett by the NVA. "Your backpack was hidden under some bamboo. The cap was still in it, so I thought I'd better bring it back or you'd be pissed at me."

"You bet your ass I would have been pissed!" Spencer tried frowning.

"Who are those guys?" Arnason pointed at the two FBI men walking up the jeep trail toward the cabin.

"Bodyguards. FBI types." Spencer shook his head.

"Up here?" Arnason felt nervous when he saw the rifle over the shoulder of the agent. "Armed?"

"Yeah . . . They think some of James's friends are going to try to kill me! I wish they *would* try!" Spencer let his anger show.

Arnason looked at Woods, who frowned back. It was getting much more serious than they had suspected. Woods was glad that they had smuggled two of their silenced .22 caliber pistols back to the States with them. At first he didn't think it was a very good idea, but now he was very glad they had done it. If the FBI thought there was a threat, there probably was one.

All five of the men sitting in the small conference room were black. The only thing that distinguished one of them from the rest was the wrinkled set of olive-drab fatigues he was wearing and the leg and arm chains. The other four men were dressed in very expensive tailor-made suits.

The soldier in chains spoke. "I don't *care* what the Supreme Minister says!" He stood up and shuffled over to the window, which was covered with a heavy screen. The smooth bolt heads were on the *inside* of the window frame, indicating that the screen was intended to keep people inside the building.

"Master Elijah is personally involved!" said the oldest man in the room.

"I don't care who's involved as long as I get out of here!" Specialist James spun around from the window and faced the four lawyers.

"That is impossible!" The senior lawyer lit a cigarette and offered it to James, who nodded. One of the junior lawyers carried the burning Kool over to where James was standing and put it in his mouth. The wrist chains were attached to a wide leather belt around his waist that prevented him from lifting his arms more than a couple of inches. "Can you have these damn chains removed!" The sentence was more of an order than a plea for help.

"You're the reason they're making you wear them. If you hadn't tried beating the guard with your shoe . . ." The lawyer looked down at James's stocking-covered feet.

"Don't make *excuses!* Do something for me besides make fucking excuses!" The cigarette in James's mouth bobbed up and down when he spoke.

"Nobody is making excuses!" The senior lawyer was becoming very angry. He really didn't want the no-win case, but the Supreme Minister had personally called and asked him to represent James. He was obligated to the Black Muslims in more ways than one. "Master Elijah *personally* sent Brother Karriem and . . ." The lawyer looked around the walls of the room for a listening device. They were in a private briefing room that had been set up for James to talk to his lawyers, but the black lawyer didn't trust the military, especially when the charges against James were considered. He nodded at one of his associates and the man opened his briefcase and turned on a small electronic box. "I feel better now." The senior lawyer smiled

"What the fuck is that?" James nodded at the black box in the briefcase.

"A modern device that prevents eavesdropping. Now listen to me, Mohammed James, because I'm only going through this *one* time." The tone of the senior lawyer's voice had changed. "You are very dangerous to the Nation—"

"Me?" James interrupted.

"Shut up and listen!" The senior lawyer's voice became extremely threatening. He nodded at one of the lawyers who had accompanied him to the military stockade that had been converted from a training POW camp at the Green Beret training area. The man unbuttoned his suit jacket and flashed a pistol in a shoulder holster at James.

"They didn't search you?" James was shocked.

"They wouldn't *dare* search your lawyers! The Army is scared shitless over this case." The lawyer placed his laced fingers on the top of the worn gray table. "We are going to exterminate the top three witnesses who can testify against you."

"Are you going to kill Spencer Barnett?" James's voice rose.

"We are going to kill *you*, if you interrupt me one more time!" The lawyer growled his words. He was becoming sick and tired of James's interruptions. "You seem to think that because you are a Death Angel you are more *special* than the rest of us!"

"I have twenty-three kills!" James hissed the words out between his teeth. His lips trembled and the long ash on his cigarette fell to the floor and burst apart.

"We *all* have kills. . . . Every man in this room is a Death Angel. I just happened to be fortunate enough to be selected for law school and the Brotherhood was kind enough to ensure the money was there to pay my tuition. . . . You think that twenty-three kills makes *you* special?"

James nodded and glared at the lawyer.

"Brother Karriem . . ." he nodded at the huge black man posing as a lawyer," has over *eighty* kills, and Brother Hassen has past fifty already." The smile on the lawyer's face was evil. "I have a considerably larger number than twenty-three, and that number isn't all devilbeasts. . . . I kill *enemies* of our Nation."

James finally understood.

The lawyer saw the change in James's expression. "Good! I knew that eventually you would understand. We will kill Barnett and the other two for you, but if that fails to prevent the military from court-martialing you . . ."

James nodded. He understood what he would have to do without the lawyer's saying it: suicide. "I'll do it, if I have to."

The lawyer tolerated the interruption. "Fine . . . as long as we understand each other. You *cannot* be tried."

James looked at the man who had given him the cigarette and with his eyes pleaded for another one. The senior lawyer nodded and the man obeyed.

"Did *anyone* ever see you eliminate a devilbeast?" The lawyer stared at James's eyes, looking for even a hint of a lie forming there.

James frowned in thought before answering. "No . . . only brother Death Angels."

"That is excellent. I can't see them being able to do anything, especially after the hearsay witnesses are dead. There won't be enough of a case to start the court-martial."

"When are you going to kill them?"

"Soon . . . very soon." The well-dressed senior lawyer stood and straightened his silk shirt. "I'll be back here the day after tomorrow with the good news."

The five black men smiled at one another. They were very good at what they did best—killing devilbeasts.

The old grandfather clock chimed twice in the hallway. Mary rolled over and reached out for Spencer. She felt his bare chest and smiled in her sleep. Spencer lay on the bed with his fingers laced behind his head. He watched the clouds cover the full moon and then move on to allow the bright light to cover the ground. He felt like going for a late night walk in the meadow to watch the deer. Spencer gently removed Mary's hand from his chest and eased out of the bed. He stepped in front of the window and picked up his Levi's from a nearby chair. The cool denim felt good against his bare skin. It was chilly outside in the mountain air, so he opened the closet door and removed a yellow-and-black-checked shirt from a hanger. It was too big for him and he had to roll up the sleeves before slipping his Levi's jacket on over it. He left the bedroom carrying his western boots in one hand.

Spencer walked down the hallway next to the wall so that he wouldn't make the floorboards squeak. He didn't want to wake up the rest of the people, especially the FBI agents. He knew that one of them would be pulling guard duty near the communications system they had installed, so he avoided the kitchen. The strong smell of freshly brewed coffee reached him at the bottom of the stairs. Staying in the shadows away from the light coming through the kitchen doorway, he eased into the den.

"Sneaking out, Spence?"

Spencer whirled around. "Shit! You scared me." He dropped down in a wing chair across from the man sitting in the shadows. A sliver of moonlight sparkled off the crystal glass he held resting on the arm of the chair. "What are you doing up so late?"

"I couldn't sleep. . . . I guess I'm still on Vietnam time." The man lifted the glass up to his shadowed head. "Arnason and Woods are on the back deck."

"Why did you guys let me sleep?"

Sergeant McDonald smiled but only a faint white glow came off his teeth in the dark room. "We didn't think you *were* sleeping up there."

Spencer smiled. "*Tonight* I was."

"Where are you going?"

"I felt like taking a walk."

"Mind if I tag along?"

"No . . . I'd like that."

McDonald stood and the moonlight slipped across half of his body. He was wearing a set of tiger cammies.

"Why the cammies?"

"Comfortable, I guess." McDonald drained his glass and reached down next to the chair. His hand came back holding one of Mary's father's shotguns. "I don't think they'll mind if we borrow this for our walk . . . would they?"

"Naw . . . if it makes you feel more comfortable." Spencer didn't need an explanation. He knew how naked he had felt in the hospital without a weapon nearby. "Did you find any shells?"

"Yes, there were a couple of boxes of slugs in the gun cabinet and three buckshot rounds."

Spencer could see the outline of a Remington ammo box in McDonald's back pocket.

"Is there an agent on duty in the kitchen?" Spencer nodded in the direction of the strong coffee smell.

"He's outside in front."

"Who made the coffee?"

"I think Arnason did."

"I'll get a mug and meet you on the back porch." Spencer went into the kitchen, blinking his eyes when he stepped into the bright light. He poured a mug of black coffee from the pot, then joined McDonald on the back porch. Arnason and Woods both nodded but didn't say anything. They had been talking with their heels resting on the railing. Woods had a light blanket covering him and his pistol in his lap. Spencer didn't realize it, but the three recon men had been pulling their own guard duty.

Spencer led the way down to the jeep trail. A loud scream that sounded like a woman echoed over the water from the lake. "Shit! What was that?"

"Loon . . . probably off its migration course." McDonald lowered the barrel of his shotgun. He had automatically pointed it.

The trail glowed in the bright moonlight. McDonald inhaled a deep breath and held it for a long time before slowly releasing it. "I could live up here."

Spencer nodded in agreement.

"How do you feel about next week?" McDonald asked, slowing his pace.

"I don't care anymore about killing James. . . . The military will punish him."

"I meant going to Washington for your medal."

Spencer shrugged. "It's all right. I don't think I deserve it, though."

"Really?"

"Fuck, I was taken prisoner by the NVA. *Real* warriors die before they let that happen."

"Do you think you're less of a man because they captured you?"

"Yes"

The old soldier and the young warrior walked down the path in silence for almost half a mile before McDonald spoke again. "You're wrong there, son."

The last word echoed in Spencer's ears.

"I'm damn proud of you, and the report Major General Garibaldi wrote up on you for the medal was nothing less than spectacular."

"He wasn't there when they captured me."

"Oh?"

"They cut off Sergeant Kirkpatrick's cock."

"And?"

"And they wiped it all over my face. . . . They wouldn't let me wash the blood off for a couple of days."

"I can't see why you feel you did something wrong."

"I should have made them kill me."

"That would have broken my heart."

Spencer stopped walking and turned to look at the old sergeant. "What?"

"I'm glad that you made it through that hell, boy. . . . You're real special and I think the military was lucky getting you."

Spencer lifted the mug of coffee to his mouth to hide his trembling upper lip.

"You can't hold yourself responsible for what the NVA did, and you surely can't feel that *you* did anything wrong when they did that to Kirkpatrick. . . . You were the victim, and God knows, boy, I feel sorry for you. Look at the other side of it: Kirk was dead when they cut off his equipment . . . it could have been worse."

"Yeah, I guess you're right."

"You did things as a POW that most men wouldn't dream of doing, and I can tell you that because you withstood torture as long as you did, a lot of NVA replacements died on the Ho Chi Minh Trail and the NVA never did have a chance to study those seismic-intrusion devices your team had planted."

Spencer slowed down and looked out over the moonlit meadow. "I know what you're trying to say, Sarge . . . but it's hard—real hard." He felt tears roll down his cheeks.

McDonald squeezed Spencer's shoulder. "I know, but don't you ever forget that there are a lot of people who care about you . . . a lot."

Spencer nodded, not trusting his voice.

"I think Mary is going to be a pretty darn good wife for you."

"Who said that we were going to get married? Hell, Sarge! I'm only seventeen years old!"

"Seventeen going on thirty!" McDonald grinned and cuffed the back of Spencer's head.

Spencer dropped down and twisted away from McDonald in a judo move and was starting to come back up when the rifle cracked. He saw the muzzle flash next to the edge of the road a hundred meters away.

McDonald dropped his shotgun and crumpled silently down in the wild flowers bordering the trail. Spencer's reaction was instant, based on months of training.

"Fuck! I missed him!" The camouflaged man lay spread-eagled next to the jeep trail.

"Dammit!" His partner also wore all black with a black ski mask pulled down over his face.

"How the fuck did I know he was going to duck like that!" The rifleman opened the bolt on his sniper rifle and ejected the spent shell. "I think I hit the guy with him, though."

"We've got to run him down before he gets back to that cabin and gets help."

Spencer low-crawled through the high grass to where McDonald lay. He felt the shotgun and checked to make sure there was a round in the chamber before looking to see if McDonald was still alive. The old NCO's eyes blinked and a bubble of red saliva formed on his lips and burst. The bullet had knocked all the air out of his lungs and he was trying to breathe.

Spencer heard the two men running toward them and raised the shotgun to his shoulder and waited. The first man had taken a couple of steps past where he was hiding before he realized it and stopped. Spencer nearly cut him in two with the first round of double-aught buckshot. The second man was ready and opened fire with his compact Uzi submachine gun. One of the rounds nicked Spencer's shin bone, sending a message of pain to his brain that he ignored. Two of the rounds smacked into Sergeant McDonald. The shock of the small-caliber rounds impacting his lower body forced the sergeant to gasp and start breathing again.

Spencer blew away the second assassin with three rapidfire rounds. The last blast forced the butt of the shotgun to press harder against his shoulder than the others had. Spencer realized that the last round had been a slug. He looked around for more of the black-suited killers and saw the trail was empty in both directions.

"Sarge?" Spencer crawled over to the Green Beret and lifted his head off the matted wild flowers.

McDonald couldn't talk and blinked his eyes to let Spencer know that he was alive.

"Sarge . . . hang in there. . . . I'll run up to the cabin and get some help." Spencer started placing McDonald's head back down on the grass when he heard Arnason and Woods running down the edge of the path through the dark trees. "Over here!" Spencer didn't know why, but he didn't yell but called out only loud enough for them to hear him.

Arnason's voice came from the opposite side of the trail. "What's going down?"

"A couple of hit men ambushed us." Spencer looked down at McDonald in his arms as he spoke.

"Where are they?"

"I killed both of them."

Arnason took a step out onto the moonlit trail. A pair of Uzis opened up from the trees on the other side of the meadow. Arnason dropped to the ground and crawled back to the nearby trees. A sharp crack of an M-16 on full automatic answered the Uzis from the head of the trail by the cabin. The FBI men were coming and their M-16s had a better range than the Uzis, which were firing wild.

Spencer rubbed McDonald's cheek and tried comforting him. McDonald gasped.

"Dad . . . don't die . . . please don't die." Spencer's subconscious mind had taken over. "Dad, I love you . . . please don't die!"

McDonald smiled. He heard Spencer but couldn't answer him. Slowly, McDonald raised his bloody hand and patted Spencer's cheek. He forced a smile and then died.

A man dressed in black stepped onto the front porch of the cabin. He had heard the rifle fire down by the meadow and figured one of his teams had run into some guards. It was an excellent distraction for his two teams.

Mary had been awakened by the shots. She felt for Spencer. He was gone, and where he had lain on the bed was cold. She realized that he had been gone for a good while. She slipped out of her white nightgown and wrapped one of her father's navy-blue bathrobes around her. She knew that her father kept a pistol in the nightstand by the bed that he used mostly to scare off raccoons that tried raiding the cabin at night. She had fired the long-barreled .44 magnum a couple of times but didn't like the kick of the large handgun. The top drawer of the nightstand stuck and she had to yank hard to get it open. The walnut handle of the blued gun came into sight just as the moonlight in the open window was blocked by a huge figure slipping into the bedroom. Mary didn't have to be told that the person was too big to be Spencer or any of his recon buddies. She removed the magnum and even took a second to pull back the hammer before she fired. The roar and flash from the gun filled the bedroom. Her father had hand loaded the rounds himself and had added extra powder because he wanted more noise than blast to scare away the animals, and he had used wadcutters for lead bullets. The force of the mushrooming lead smashed Brother Karriem back through the window. His huge shoulder caught a corner of the window frame and split the wood on his journey back down to the ground.

Mary recocked the hammer and slipped out of the bedroom into the hallway. She saw the light from the kitchen at the foot of the stairs and thought better of exposing herself. She squatted next to one of the guest-bedroom doors and tipped a ceramic vase over on its side and rolled it over the carpet so that it would bounce down the steps. The vase thudded down the stairs and shattered when it hit the oak floor.

The bright flashes coming from an Uzi lit up the dark wall of the den opposite the open balcony where Mary now squatted. She stuck the barrel of the .44 magnum between two of the rails and fired a little above the flashes. The lights jerked and went out. Mary heard the body hit the floor and then it was quiet in the cabin.

Arnason reached the back porch a couple of steps ahead of Woods. They each carried a silenced pistol. Arnason used the barrel of his gun to point with, and Woods nodded and slipped around to circle the cabin. A dark shadow rose from behind a lounge chair and both of the recon men fired. The drama was played like a mime, without any noise being made. The shadow slumped down over the padded lounge chair. The roar of the magnum inside the cabin made Arnason jump. He saw a flash coming from an Uzi in the den and then another loud roar.

Woods held his pistol in both hands and used the whole barrel to line up on the running figure before he fired in the moonlight. The figure stumbled and dropped down to one knee before getting back up on its feet to hobble into the dark trees.

Arnason pushed open the French doors and eased down next to the foot-thick log wall. "Mary?"

"Yes?"

"Are you all right?"

"I think so . . ."

"I'm coming in through the French doors."

"Okay."

Arnason slipped into the den and did a forward roll on the rug before coming to a stop in front of the leather couch.

"I don't think there are any more inside the cabin." Mary's voice came from the landing above the den.

"Stay where you are and let me check it out." Arnason started going through all the rooms, avoiding the bright light coming from the kitchen.

"The house is clear." Arnason stood at the foot of the stairs and waited for Mary to come down. His eyes widened when he saw the huge magnum in the tiny nurse's hand.

"Where's Spencer Barnett?" Worry filled her voice.

"He's fine . . . he's down on the trail with two of the FBI agents."

"Has he been hurt? I heard shots—that's why I got Daddy's gun out."

"He's fine . . . but Sergeant McDonald's been hit."

"Let me get my first-aid kit and we can go down there." Mary didn't wait for Arnason to answer. He knew it would be impossible to prevent her from going to Spencer, and besides, he wasn't going to screw with her as long as she held that hand cannon.

Spencer was still holding McDonald in his arms and rocking gently back and forth when Mary and Arnason appeared on the jeep trail. The FBI agents had left to call for help as soon as they realized that Arnason and Woods were armed and Barnett wasn't about to leave the dead sergeant.

Mary dropped down next to Spencer and took McDonald's wrist. She felt for a pulse and found none. Spencer's face was streaked from tears that had washed channels in the blood McDonald had wiped there. She hugged him and started crying too. "My dear . . . dear Spencer Barnett."

Master Elijah watched his tarantulas in his hundred-gallon terrarium. He held the telephone loosely to his ear as if the instrument were getting too hot to hold. The expression on his face became gloomier the longer he listened. He rubbed his chin with his free hand and then hung up the telephone without saying a word.

The man standing in the shadows of the room stepped forward and waited until the Supreme Minister spoke. "We've lost four Death Angels tonight and the mission failed."

The female tarantula touched the clean glass with her pedipalps. The minister tapped the outside of the glass with the eight-carat canary-yellow diamond ring he wore on his right pinkie. "Kill him."

The man left the minister without saying a word. He smiled as he walked down the hallway to the rear parking lot of the Detroit mosque. He was going to enjoy the drive to North Carolina in his new canary-yellow Seville.

The shrill sound of a mountain blue jay echoed through the air. No one at the cabin paid any attention to the bird. The special team that had flown to the cabin from Washington, D.C., had deployed throughout the whole wooded area and two A-teams of Green Berets were due to arrive from Fort Bragg before noon.

The agent in charge looked down at the four bodies lying in the shade of the rear deck of the cabin. All of the men were black and dressed in identical black uniforms. There wasn't any more doubt left that a secret black sect was involved with Specialist James and that they wanted to kill the witnesses who could testify against him. Like all bureaucracies, somebody had to die before the sect took the necessary precautions.

Spencer Barnett sat on the ground next to a body that was wrapped in a Hudson Bay blanket. He had his back to the cabin and looked out over the lake. Mary and his teammates watched from the railing surrounding the deck. They could feel his pain but were absolutely incapable of removing it. Spencer reached over and touched the white portion of the blanket where Sergeant McDonald's hand was, then stood up with his back still to the cabin. His lips moved as he silently pledged revenge.

CHAPTER SIX

The Rose Garden

The funeral for Master Sergeant Jeremiah McDonald drew over five hundred active-duty and retired Special Forces men and another two hundred officers and senior enlisted men from the Pentagon and Fort Meyers to his grave site in Arlington National Cemetery.

Corporal Barnett stood on the right-hand side of the grave and received the triangular folded flag that had been removed from the top of the casket by the sergeant major who led the Special Forces honor guard. McDonald's wife and teenage son had been killed in an automobile accident right before he went to Vietnam; some people said that was the reason he had volunteered for duty over there and then had volunteered again to serve on Project Cherry, a suicide unit that had been designed for POW snatches. Spencer had been listed by the sergeant as his next of kin and benefactor for all his insurance policies.

Mary's hand started quivering as she held tightly to Spencer's arm when a hidden bugler started playing taps. The extremely sad notes from the bugle slipped between the mounds of freshly dug soil that dotted the bright green lawns. Vietnam was giving the caretakers at the huge cemetery a lot of overtime pay. Handkerchiefs came out of the rear pockets of many AG-44 dress uniforms during the slow rendition of the hand salute to the fallen warrior by the members of the honor guard.

Woods glanced over at Spencer out of the corner of his eye without moving his head and saw that his war buddy was standing ramrod straight with his eyes looking down at the dull bronze military-issue casket. Woods noticed that the expression on Spencer's face was one of deep concentration and a little wonder mixed in around the corners of his eyes. Spencer's natural curls at the corners of his mouth would have been misinterpreted as the beginning of a smile by anyone who didn't know him.

The bugler finished the rendition of taps and the cemetery became absolutely quiet. Then horns and the hum of traffic on the nearby highway slowly filled the silence. Spencer handed the folded flag to Mary and leaned over to pull back a corner of the imitation grass carpet that was used to hide the pile of grave dirt from the mourners.

Spencer turned around so that Arnason and Woods could hear him. "Warriors bury their own dead." The statement was made in a very soft voice but it carried to the first couple of rows circling the grave. He reached down and dug up a handful of rich black soil and dropped it onto the casket. The hollow sound of the dirt clods hitting the metal box filled the hole in the earth. Arnason and Woods were next. Mary handed the flag back to Spencer and dug up a double handful of the pleasant-smelling soil and dropped it onto the growing mound.

The word spread through the crowd and a line formed to walk past the grave, with each soldier, woman, and child stopping to drop a handful of dirt on the warrior's remains. A tradition that was ancient in the old country had been reborn in America, but with a powerful new twist. The handful of dirt wasn't symbolic anymore but was an actual burial. When the mourners had finished filing past the grave, there wasn't enought dirt left for the grave diggers even to have to clean up. Master Sergeant Jeremiah McDonald had been buried by other warriors and by people who loved and admired him.

Lieutenant Colonel Martin left his place by the row of gravestones from which he had been observing Spencer and started walking toward the small clods of dirt that remained, but stopped when he caught the look in Spencer's eyes. He shrugged, rationalizing that the grave was already filled and didn't need any more earth. The Walter Reed Army Hospital psychiatrist noticed that none of the Special Forces soldiers had wiped or brushed the streaks of dirt off their hands, but then again, it was his job to notice unique or unusual things about human behavior. The lieutenant colonel had come to the funeral to observe how Spencer would handle the additional burden of losing a close friend, not because he had cared about the senior NCO. Spencer had sensed that and tolerated the psychiatrist's presence only to keep the peace.

Spencer remained standing next to the grave while the crowd started moving back to their cars and buses.

"Spence, we'd better leave. . . ." Woods was one of the few men there who dared speak to Spencer. "We've got to be at the White House in less than an hour."

"He died so . . . so *simply.*" Spencer kept staring at the mound of earth. "I mean, he should have died like a hero . . . in Vietnam. You know, with a couple of dozen NVA piled up around him!" Spencer's voice started to rise.

"Look around you, Spence" Arnason squeezed his recon teammate's shoulder. "He *is* a hero, and when he died, he was near someone he loved a lot." Arnason shook his head once from side to side and added, "You can't ask for much more than that when your time comes." Arnason's thoughts went back to the long planning meetings he had attended with McDonald for the POW snatch mission that was going into Laos for Spencer and the Air Force colonel. He knew how fanatically McDonald had worked and could still recall the look in McDonald's eyes every time he had glanced at the eight-by-ten glossy photograph of Barnett that had been placed on the briefing-room wall along with those of the Colonel Garibaldi and Specialist James.

It was almost imperceptible, but Spencer gave a curt nod of agreement and spoke. "Okay, let's go or they'll get even more pissed at me."

Woods smiled to himself at Spencer's statement. Spencer had told the White House aide that he would be a half hour late for his presentation because he had to attend the funeral of a friend. There had been a mad scramble in the Pentagon and the White House and finally the President had changed his schedule so that Spencer could be present at the grave site.

Spencer paused in the open door of the military sedan and looked back at the lonely grave. One of the gravediggers was tidying up the site. He smiled and then gave a quick wink before sliding down along the seat. Mary had caught the gesture and smiled herself; it was as if Spencer had just talked with McDonald and something funny had been said between them.

The national press corps was already assembled in the Rose Garden when the sedan carrying Spencer and Mary pulled up under the arched entrance. Arnason and Woods had been dropped off in the spectator section where they could observe the presentation with the other military guests. Spencer was rushed into a side entrance of the White House by a military aide and Mary was escorted to a chair off to one side of the sunny flowered area where a number of senior dignitaries' wives were waiting.

"Corporal Barnett, we'd like for you to wait in her until the President is ready." The Army colonel began briefing Spencer on the ceremony. "It will be short and simple, with the President making the presentation. All you have to do is come to attention and tilt your head a little forward so the President can place the medal around your neck. You will be the only recipient today for the medal." The colonel paused, trying to allow the significance of the solitary presentation to sink into the young soldier's mind. When he saw that it wasn't fazing Spencer, he continued, "Senator Strom Thurmond from South Carolina will say a few words in your honor and General Westmoreland will make a couple of comments about your service in Vietnam before everyone will come into the *small* reception room for coffee and cake . . . compliments of the President. Do you have any questions?" The colonel was becoming very angry because Spencer was not responding to the special honors that were being bestowed on him. It was very rare that General Westmoreland was back in the States and even rarer for him to have time for small ceremonies. The colonel had been privy to Spencer's files and saw why they were making a special effort for the boy-soldier from South Carolina. The kid was the kind of material that *hometown* heroes were made of, and with the growing hippie and anti-war movement, the government needed another Audie Murphy.

The colonel felt jealousy growing inside him and snapped, "Well? Do you have any questions?"

Spencer looked directly in the senior officer's eyes and slowly shook his head in the negative.

"Fine. Wait here until I come back to get you." The colonel started to leave, then stopped. "That's an order."

Spencer smiled and walked over to a tall window that overlooked the Rose Garden and looked out. He clasped his hands behind his back and slipped into his own private world of thoughts.

A set of French doors opened and a man in his late fifties stepped into the high-ceilinged, ornate room. He saw the young soldier standing in the window light and paused on his way out of the side exit, then returned to where the soldier was standing.

"Excuse me, young man, but aren't you the soldier who's going to receive the Medal of Honor today?"

As Spencer turned to face the soft voice, the bright sunlight rested on the four rows of ribbons that covered the chest and upper left side of his uniform.

"You've got more medals there, son, than most of the officers I've met." The man's smile was genuine.

Spencer smiled back. "I picked up a couple." He looked down at his chest as if he were just noticing for the first time that he possessed most of the nation's valor awards.

"I'm Ronald Reagan, governor of California."

"California?"

"Yep . . ." The man's smile widened. "Have you ever been there?"

Spencer shook his head slowly. "Just long enough to pass through . . . thank God."

Governor Reagan's eyebrows lifted. "Why do you say that? We've got a mighty fine state. . . ."

"Too much dope for this kid." Spencer grinned. "You've

got to clean that up, Governor, because it's geting pretty bad over in Vietnam."

"Are you blaming California?"

The look in Spencer's eyes told the governor that the young soldier was.

"Well . . . I'm doing my best to clean up a lot of things in California."

Spencer nodded in agreement.

"You sure do speak what's on your mind, don't you." Governor Reagan smiled again. He was intrigued with the honesty of the young man—a trait that was almost extinct in Washington. "What do you think of the draft?"

"It's good." Spencer turned his head slightly to the left so that the warm rays of the sun would touch his cheek. The feeling comforted him. "As long as it's fair and everyone's number is put in the hat."

"Yes . . . I guess you've got a point there." Governor Reagan saw his aide hurrying toward the doors. "Well, I've got a meeting with the President right after your award ceremony." A very wide grin spread out on the man's face. "I was in there earlier when the call came in that you were going to attend your sergeant's funeral. I must say that the conversation would have to have been censored if it had been televised. You've got guts, young man, and I admire that . . . loyalty too, and that's a rare trait." The governor nodded toward his waving aide. "If you're ever in California, look me up." He handed Spencer an engraved business card with a private telephone number on it. "Call that number and one of my aides will know what to do to reach me."

Spencer kept looking down at the card. "Thanks! I might do that sometime if I ever want to learn how to surf!"

Reagan chuckled. "We've enough surfers in California to take care of you. Good luck, young man."

"Thank you, Governor . . ." Spencer flashed one of his best smiles, "and I hope you make President someday!"

"Thanks, but California is enough for one man to handle!" Governor Reagan started his brisk business walk the instant he slipped through the double doors. Spencer watched him disappear down the wide hallway with his aide. Both men were talking with their hands as they hurried toward the conference room.

Spencer returned his attention to the gathered reporters outside the window. He could see Mary sitting with the wives and smiled to himself because she looked out-of-place among all the gray-haired ladies.

"Corporal Barnett? Are you ready to join us?" A brigadier general poked his head through the doorway.

"Yes sir." Spencer checked his reflection in a nearby mirror and adjusted his tie before following the general outside into the Rose Garden. Everyone there was staring at him and a barrage of flashbulbs erupted in his face. Spencer swallowed and felt a very unfamiliar nervousness start to form in the pit of his stomach. He wasn't going to like all this attention.

He saw the proud smile first and recognized the rest of the man standing in the crowd afterward. Spencer stopped walking behind the general and stared over the thick nylon rope that separated the spectators from the invited guests. He took the half-dozen steps to the place where the man stood with his wife and teenage son.

"What . . . what are *you* doing here?" Spencer was almost stuttering.

"A Sergeant Woods called us down in South Carolina and told us that you were in the Army and would be getting the Medal of Honor today. . . . You know we wouldn't have missed being here for anything."

"But you didn't even try to find me . . . *five* years!"

The man's wife cut in," That's not true, Spencer! He was thrown in jail for thirty days because he caused the social-services people so much hell!"

"Believe me, Spence, I tried, but they hid you from us and even snuck you into the Army without us knowing!"

Spencer could see in the man's eyes that he wasn't lying. He looked at his foster brother and smiled. "We've got to go coon hunting again . . . soon!"

"Promise?" The fourteen-year-old's eyes lit up.

"That's a promise!"

"Corporal Barnett? We're waiting," said the Army colonel assigned to military protocol. The brigadier general had his hand on the colonel's arm and smiled. The colonel looked at the general and understood that Spencer had made another friend. "If you don't mind," he added.

"I'll see you'all later." Spencer smiled and felt a long-established hurt disappear. His foster parents hadn't dumped him as he had been told by the social-services staff. "How did you get here?"

"Sergeant Woods paid for our air fare."

Spencer smiled. He owed David a lot for this.

Spencer had loved living with the Callam family when he was a foster child in the South Carolina social-services program. They were the first *real* family he had ever seen where love and respect for one another were basic parts of family life.

Camera strobe lights flashed, bringing Spencer back to the White House Rose Garden. Even the Army colonel realized that something special had gone on between the boy-hero and the family from South Carolina.

The Army's "Caisson" song echoed against the white stucco of the building the instant Corporal Barnett's foot touched the carpeted patio. Members from the Old Guard Division's band played the music they knew by heart. Spencer stood where the brigadier general pointed on the red carpet and looked back at the French doors. His thoughts slipped back to Arlington Cemetery.

Sergeant Arnason felt a shiver ripple down his spine. The air seemed to transmit excitement. He felt that everything in front of him would vanish if he blinked his eyes. Some of the most powerful men in America were casually talking to one another around the Rose Garden as they waited for the President to appear and make the presentation. Arnason recognized General Westmoreland talking to Senator Thurmond from South Carolina.

"Hail to the Chief" began abruptly by the band as the President of the United States emerged from his residence, followed by a half-dozen Treasury agents and aides. Everyone in the Rose Garden watched as he approached the blond boy-hero from South Carolina. Spencer's foster mother started crying and her husband and son slipped their arms around her.

Spencer watched the President approach and at the last possible second the most powerful man in America smiled at the soldier, but the smile didn't reach his eyes. Spencer looked away and blinked before searching the gathered crowd for a friendly face. He found Arnason and Woods and smiled at them. It looked like they were really enjoying themselves.

A voice coming from a hidden loudspeaker system stopped the music and small talk within the crowd. "Ladies and gentlemen . . . the President of the United States."

"Thank you very much for joining us here in the Rose Garden for this very special occasion. We have gathered here to honor one of our Vietnam War heroes . . ." the President glanced down at the three-by-five card in his hand, "Corporal Spencer Barnett from the great state of South Carolina." He glanced up at Senator Thurmond and smiled; the senator was the senior member of the powerful Armed Services Committee. "Corporal Barnett has earned this nation's highest military award for distinguishing himself conspicuously by gallantry and intrepidity at the risk of his life. . . ." The President glanced down at the card again, then looked over at the closed doors leading into the White House. A professional-sounding voice came back on over the hidden speakers to read the official citation:

> "Corporal Spencer Barnett, while serving as a long-range reconnaissance team member with the first Cavalry Division in Vietnam, distinguished himself by numerous acts of valor and courage at the risk of his life while engaged with and armed enemy of the United States of America.
>
> Corporal Barnett engaged a large enemy force along with other members of his team in the A Shau Valley of Vietnam and he personally killed or wounded fourteen enemy soldiers before ordering his teammates to withdraw while he provided protective fire. The large enemy force overran Corporal Barnett's position and captured him along with another member of his reconnaissance team.
>
> Corporal Barnett was tortured by the enemy in the most cruel manner and yet he still wouldn't divulge the top-secret information he possessed, which resulted in the direct elimination of over four hundred fifty-three North Vietnamese combat soldiers. . . ."

Sergeant Arnason tried reading Spencer's face but could see only a blank stare. The President was sweeping the crowd with his eyes, smiling and nodding his head at political friends and foes alike.

> ". . . The enemy increased their various tortures and yet Corporal Barnett refused to reveal the location of sensitive secret equipment, even though others had broken under the extreme torture and compromised the information.
>
> Corporal Barnett conducted himself honorably and with great courage that reflects highly on his unit, his country, and himself. . . ."

The narrator's voice droned on, impressing even the most hardened military men in the crowd. Corporal Barnett's citation read like a Hollywood cult-hero movie.

Spencer's thoughts were on Mary. He kept staring over at her and could see the extreme pride in her eyes, which made him happy. A military aide took two sharp steps forward and opened the blue leather box for the President. The beautiful light blue neck ribbon glittered in the bright light against the tan background in the box. The President removed the medal and held it up in the air for a second so that the cameramen could take pictures of him holding it, then he placed it around Spencer's neck. The Old Guard band began playing "America the Beautiful."

Woods leaned over and whispered in Arnason's ear, "Shit! this is making me jealous!"

Arnason smiled and whispered back, "Me too!"

The ceremony was well done and everything was executed perfectly. Spencer was escorted back to the small reception room for coffee and cake by the President, who excused himself shortly thereafter to attend an important meeting.

Mary went to Spencer and hugged him. "You looked wonderful standing up there!"

"Sure . . ." Spencer blushed. "I'd rather have been with you in the meadow. . . ." Mary blushed.

"What are you two talking about that's making your faces turn red?" Woods grabbed his buddy's hand and shook it. "Congratulations!"

"Thanks." Spencer hugged Mary.

"Well, now that you've won The Big One, you can retire." Arnason shook hands with Spencer.

"What do you mean *retire?*" Spencer was still smiling. "You know—Medal of Honor winners are never sent back to combat . . . it has something to do with everyone, including themselves, expecting too much from them." Arnason watched the color drain from Spencer's face. "You weren't planning on going back there . . . were you?"

"Yes . . . yes I was." Spencer couldn't believe what he had just heard. "You mean I can't serve in any *future* wars?"

"Maybe, if the President himself signed your orders." Arnason was being facetious but Spencer took him seriously.

"Whew! I thought there for a second that there was no way I could get back to Vietnam. Hell, if that was the case, I surely wouldn't have accepted this medal." Spencer smiled.

Woods shook his head and Arnason started laughing. "Spencer, what the hell are we going to do with you!" He turned to Mary. "Woman! Mellow this guy out for us, will you!"

"I'm trying . . . Lord knows I'm trying!" She started laughing too.

The next hour was filled with senior military officers and NCOs congratulating Spencer and people staring at the medal hanging around his neck. Spencer ignored the stares and enjoyed his friends and the members of his foster family. The fourteen-year-old kept reaching up to touch the medal.

"Would you like to try it on?" Spencer started reaching behind his neck to unfasten the ribbon.

"Please!" The Army colonel appeared suddenly. "Don't insult the United States Army by letting a kid wear our highest award in public!"

Spencer glared at the colonel and was stopped from saying what was on the tip of his tongue by Arnason's hand squeezing his arm. "He's right, Spence . . . someone might get *jealous* if you let the boy wear it here in front of the press."

Spencer glared at the staff colonel for another couple of seconds, then said to the fourteen-year-old, with his eyes still on the officer, "You can wear it later."

"If you would please exit through the side doors soon, I

will be able to get the rest of the people to leave and have this room cleaned up for the next event for today." The colonel kept his eyes averted as he spoke.

Woods nodded toward the door. "Let's go." He waited until they were on the walkway headed toward their sedans before adding, "What an ass!"

"The Army is made up of all kinds of people," Arnason replied as he stepped into a waiting car. He rolled down the window and called over to Spencer, who was riding with Mary, "I think we're all going over to the Washington Sheraton for the rest of the day and then fly back to the cabin tomorrow."

Spencer nodded in agreement. He had been briefed that they would be staying in special reserved suites at the Washington, D.C., hotel for the night so that Spencer could meet with his family and friends, and then they would return to the cabin for a couple of days before flying by Army helicopter to Camp McCall for the opening of James's court-martial.

It was raining in Detroit, which made the funeral ceremony for the four Death Angels even more dreary. Master Elijah stood under a large black umbrella that was being held by a twelve-year-old acolyte. The boy had green eyes and medium-brown skin and did not adhere to the pure racial standards that Elijah had personally set for acolytes to the Brotherhood, but he had made an exception in the boy's case to show his congregation that even diluted black blood was stronger than pure white blood. The boy suffered from a great deal of harassment by the *pure* black acolytes attending classes at the mosque, but Master Elijah could see that it was making the boy tougher. He would never admit even to the child that he was very partial to him, especially the child's fine features and soft wavy hair. The boy could easily have been a high-paid model in any agency in Detroit. Master Elijah looked out over the crowd surrounding the four closed caskets, then paused to look at the boy's face before returning his attention to the assembled ministers standing in a row to the right of the caskets. He smiled pleasantly to himself as he considered what they would think if they knew that the mixed-blood acolyte standing next to him was his son by one of his white mistresses.

The minister from the mosque in Atlanta looked around the gathering in the cemetery for his bodyguards. He didn't like standing so long out in the open, especially in a downtown Detroit cemetery. He located his men and nodded toward his limousine. He wanted them to be ready to leave the instant the burial was finished. He sneaked a glaring look over at Master Elijah and was caught by the penetrating glare of the Supreme Minister. It was too late for him to change the expression on his face, so he allowed his hate to show through. He, along with all the other ministers from around the country, had told Master Elijah that it would be stupid to all show up together for the funeral of the four Death Angels, but Master Elijah had insisted that they appear together as a show of unity to the congregation. He was sure that very few people inside the church knew that the Death Angels even existed, and those who weren't Death Angels or pledged to become Death Angels had no idea of what they really did for the mosque leaders. The word had been spread through the congregation that the deaths were due to a drug war between the Brotherhood and the devilbeasts.

The two black FBI agents blended in perfectly with the crowd standing around the caskets. They wore modest business suits and tan raincoats. A team of special photographers was set up on the roof of a large warehouse across the street from the Brotherhood. When they returned to their headquarters and developed the photographs, they would be in for a very pleasant surprise. The leader from Atlanta had passed out to each Death Angel present at the funeral a small silver angel earring to wear in honor of their fallen comrades. Master Elijah had forbidden even mentioning association with the Death Angels outside of the mosques and would have had the minister shot on the spot if he had known about the earrings. The FBI agents would notice the silver angels and within a few weeks identify all of them as criminals wanted for other crimes.

* * *

Spencer Barnett looked out of the seventh-floor window at the darkening sky. He held a glass of Coke in his hand. Mary approached him from behind and wrapped her arms around his waist. He smiled and turned around to hug her. "Thanks for coming today. I needed to see your face there."

"It was my pleasure, Spencer Barnett." She kissed him.

"Please!" Woods set his beer down on the glass coffee table and exaggerated with his hands. "Wait until I leave for my R and R back in Nebraska before you cause me to bust!"

Mary smiled shyly. "For you, David . . . we'll wait."

Spencer glanced over at his foster brother, who had fallen asleep curled up on the dark maroon sofa in the luxury suite. The fourteen-year-old was wearing Spencer's Medal of Honor around his neck and held the medallion clenched tightly in his hand.

"We'd better get him back to our motel room." The father set his finished drink down on the bar and looked over at his wife.

"Where are you staying?" The tone in Spencer's voice told the Callams that he didn't want them to leave.

"Somewhere down the street a piece . . . The Mayflower?" The man looked at his wife, who nodded.

"Look . . . I've got a double suite here. . . ." Spencer went over to the double doors that led off the main living area and opened them to reveal a large double bed and a private bath. "You can use this bedroom and I still have mine on the other side." Spencer nodded at the double doors opposite the ones he had opened.

"I don't know . . . bothering you with all of your friends . . ."

"You're *not* bothering us," Arnason said, coming to Spencer's rescue. "We're living just down the hall a piece, so in fact we'll be bothering you."

The father looked down at his sleeping son. "He's all tuckered out and I hate to move him. . . ."

"Then it's settled! You'll stay with us tonight!" Spencer was happy. He needed to have family around him.

"Well, seeing's that we're not traveling tonight, Mother . . ." The father picked up his glass and held it in the air. The pleading look in his eyes brought a smile to his wife's face.

"If you mind yourself and don't make a fool out of the Callam family name!"

"I feel a good drunk coming on!" The father chuckled and went back to the bar.

"While you're drinking all of Spencer's liquor, I might as well go over to the other hotel and get our things." She looked at her son and smiled. "He'll sleep until next Sunday if we let him, and then he'll be mad for a week because he's missed everything. . . . Pa, you'd better wake him up."

"In a minute . . ." The father poured his glass three-quarters full of Wild Turkey. It had been almost a year since he'd put on a good drunk, telling stories with friends, and he was looking forward to it.

Arnason stood up and stretched. "I think I'll tag along with Mrs. Callam, if she doesn't mind." The look Arnason flashed to Woods told him that he would watch the woman and that Woods should stick with Spencer. The FBI had agents covering every entrance to the whole wing they occupied and Arnason knew that the woman wouldn't be allowed to return unless she was escorted.

Woods nodded his agreement and winked.

Spencer refilled his glass with ice cubes and Coke and leaned over to whisper in Woods's ear, "Did anyone ask my mother to come today?"

Woods felt his stomach knot before he answered. "She wanted to come, but your stepfather wouldn't let her."

Spencer clenched his jaws and went back to sit next to Mary. He couldn't hide from her the hurting inside and she gently ran her fingers through the hair on the back of his neck. He felt a burning desire to make love to her to hide the hurt he was feeling. She sensed his need and nodded toward the closed bedroom door.

Spencer looked at Woods, who nodded for him to leave. "Your foster father and I can keep each other company for *two* minutes . . . go ahead."

Spencer reverted to his old self. "Two minutes! We'll see! You are talking to a South Carolina–bred boy now!"

"*Boy* is right!" Woods laughed.

"Those are fighting words, David!"

Mary tugged at Spencer's arm. "What do you want to do . . . make love or war?"

Spencer paused, and an expression of great dilemma was exaggerated on his face.

Mary swatted his arm. "Spencer Barnett! If you don't—"

"Love . . . let's make love." He started laughing and slipped into the bedroom behind Mary. The door opened as soon as it had closed and Spencer pointed his finger at David and mouthed the word *WAR!*

Woods laughed along with the foster father, who made a very appropriate remark: "It's hard not to love that boy."

Spencer lay on the bed with his arm around Mary. She was sleeping deeply from the exhausting day's events. He looked out the window at the reflected lights coming up from the brightly lit entrance to the hotel. He had been lying there awake for hours. He knew what he had to do and got out of bed to get dressed. The zipper on his suitcase seemed to sound like a train as he opened the case and removed a pair of Levi's and a checkered flannel shirt. He left his western boots in the suitcase and removed his Reebok running shoes instead. He needed footwear that was practical in case he had to run.

The door to his bedroom opened quietly and he slipped out into the living room of the suite. His foster brother was still sleeping on the couch, with the medal around his neck. Spencer gently tried to unlatch the medal, but the boy woke up.

"Shhhh . . ." Spencer placed the palm of his hand over the fourteen-year-old's mouth and then removed it. "I need to borrow that medal for a little while."

"Sure, Spence . . ." The boy reached behind his neck and unlatched the clasp. He handed the medal to his hero, who was only a little more than three years older than he was. "Where are you going, Spence?"

"To visit a friend." Spencer placed the Medal of Honor in its box and tucked it away in his shirt.

"Can I come along?" the boy whispered.

Spencer shook his head no and went to the bar. He hopped up on the Formica top and pushed up against one of the decorative plastic panels suspended from the ceiling. The panel moved easily and Spencer stuck his head up through the opening. It was exactly as he had hoped: the false lowered ceiling opened up wide enough for a man to crawl between it and the roof. He looked back at his foster brother sitting on the couch and saw the hurt look in his eyes. Spencer smiled and nodded for the boy to join him. The fourteen-year-old hurried to slip on his tennis shoes and hopped up on the bar with Spencer.

"You've got to be super quiet so that we don't get caught." Spencer pulled himself up through the opening and moved over so the boy could join him.

The roof creaked slightly but not enough to alert the FBI agents who were on guard outside the suite. Spencer and his foster brother crawled all the way over to the opposite wing of the hotel floor, then Spencer removed another of the lightweight ceiling panels and dropped down into the hallway, followed by his partner. The excitement in the boy's eyes told Spencer that the kid didn't care why they were sneaking out or, for that matter, where they were going.

Spencer adjusted the case tucked in his shirt and hurried down the fire-exit stairs to the ground floor of the hotel. He paused at the exit and searched the corridor both ways before exiting. He was sure that the FBI would have even the ground floor of the hotel watched. They slipped out of the building and Spencer led the way back to a side street where they caught a taxi.

Spencer leaned forward and spoke through the holes in the Plexiglas that separated the driver from the passengers. "Arlington Cemetery, please."

The driver looked back at him as if he were crazy. It was two o'clock in the morning. "The place is chained shut."

"Take us to one of the side gates." Spencer smiled. "For an extra ten bucks?"

"Done!" The driver slipped the old taxi into gear and turned onto Massachusetts Avenue.

Spencer looked up at the tall iron gate in the dark. The thick black bars would be easy to climb. He looked over at his foster brother. "You think you can make it?"

"Sure!" The boy grabbed hold of the bars and was up and over the fence before Spencer had gotten a decent foothold. "Why do we want to come here at night?" The excitement was still present in his voice. He was loving the adventure.

"Like I said, to see a friend." Spencer looked around for a couple of minutes before he decided which direction to take in the large cemetery and then started walking at a fast pace. His foster brother kept close to him, not that he was scared or anything like that, for he was a country boy from South Carolina and they weren't scared of anything, except maybe a haunt or two.

Spencer saw the raised mound of fresh earth in the dark and looked around again. He recognized a large tomb in the background and was sure of where he was. He dropped back down on his rear in the loose soil and smiled. "Hi, Sarge . . . I brought my little brother with me to see you."

The fourteen-year-old's teeth gleamed brightly in the moonlight.

"I thought you might want to see this, too." Spencer unbuttoned his shirt and removed the case. The moonlight reflected off the Medal of Honor. "Have you ever seen one of these before?" Spencer paused as if he were being answered and then added, "Me neither, until today."

The fourteen-year-old took a seat on the damp grass and listened to the one-sided conversation between Spencer and the grave. Anyone else who might have been there would have thought the young soldier had gone totally crazy, but the boy figured if Spencer wanted to talk out loud to a grave, that was his business; after all, he talked to his black-and-tan hounds all the time and he knew *he* wasn't crazy.

Spencer talked for over an hour to the sergeant's grave, telling the dead warrior about his plans with Mary and asking his opinion a half-dozen times about what he should do. Each time Spencer asked a question, he paused as though listening to an answer.

Mary woke up and found Spencer missing. She looked over at the bathroom door and didn't see any light around its edges. She listened for conversation in the living room but heard nothing. Fear burst in her heart and she rushed from the bed.

The suite was empty. She ran to the telephone and dialed Woods's number. It rang only once before he picked it up.

"Hello?" There wasn't any sleep in his voice.

"David, is Spencer with you?"

"No . . ." Caution filled the sergeant's voice.

"How about with Arnason?"

"He's here."

"David, Spencer is missing!"

"Have you checked the rest of the suite?"

"Yes!"

"How about the Callams' room?"

"No . . . But the boy is gone too!"

"Unlock the door—we'll be right there!" David hung up the telephone, followed Arnason out of the room, and reached the suite before Mary could walk over and unlock the door. The two FBI agents on duty saw the concern on the sergeants' faces and started walking toward them.

"Where do you think he went?" Mary's voice was near panicking.

"The boy is with him. Spencer probably took him downstairs for a midnight snack in the lounge." Arnason was trying to calm her down as his eyes searched the room.

"The guards outside would know." Mary opened the door and asked the agents if they had seen Spencer leave the suite. Both of the FBI men became extremely alert. The senior man called an alert over his hand-held radio.

"Don't worry, Mary. . . ." Woods walked over to the bar and looked behind it. "Spencer would never endanger the boy. He's nearby." David saw the loose fiber dust on the bar top and looked up. He noticed that the ceiling panel directly above the bar was slightly raised in one corner. Spencer had left through the roof. He nodded at Arnason and then up at the ceiling. The recon sergeant picked up instantly what Woods was telling him.

The room filled with a dozen agents who began searching all the closets and waking the Callams to search their room. The senior agent approached Arnason. "Do you know where he might have gone?"

Arnason put his arm over Mary's shoulder and hugged her. "I'm pretty sure I can find him."

"Please! Let's go!" The agent's voice was urgent. He had read the secret Agency reports and knew that the soldier's life was in extreme danger. Teams of black hit men had been searching the Washington area trying to locate the hotel or residence where Spencer and the other witnesses were being kept.

Spencer was still sitting on the damp mound of earth talking to his sergeant when the headlights lit up the narrow asphalt road leading back into the cemetery. He stood up and brushed the seat of his Levi's before slipping the medal back inside his shirt. His foster brother rose and looked at Spencer's face, trying to determine if he should run or stay there.

The lead-car door opened and Arnason stepped out of one side while the agent jumped out of the other.

"Hi, Spence... You ready to come back now?" Arnason walked slowly toward Master Sergeant McDonald's grave.

"Yeah, we were just about done."

"What were you doing out here?" The FBI agent swept the gravestones with his eyes as he spoke.

"Talking to a friend," Spencer's foster brother answered the FBI agent.

CHAPTER SEVEN

Court-Martial

There wasn't even a breeze to move the hot, humid air outside the small wooden buildings at Camp McCall. Arnason had carried one of the large military fans outside and had it blowing over the stained redwood picnic table they were all sitting around under a stand of loblolly pine. The three of them were wearing T-shirts to absorb their sweat, but they had removed their khaki short-sleeved shirts to keep them from getting wrinkled and sweat stained.

Woods ran his finger down the side of his Coke can and watched as the condensation was absorbed almost instantly into the dry wood. "When do you think they'll call us?"

Arnason twisted his mouth before answering, "This shit can go on forever."

"Where do you think they're keeping James?" The tone in Spencer's voice was deadly.

Arnason stared across the table at Spencer and could see that there was more on his mind than just testifying at James's court-martial. "Spence . . . we've got to let the Army handle James!"

Barnett slowly turned his head so that he could look directly at his recon team sergeant. The look in his eyes made the recon sergeant shiver; even the natural curls at the corners of

Spencer's mouth looked demonic. "I *am* going to let the Army handle him." Spencer tried smiling but the effect was lost when it reached his eyes. "Why wouldn't I?"

Lieutenant Colonel Martin stepped through the open back door of the barracks that led out to the picnic area. A wooden privacy wall had been erected by the Special Forces Training Detachment years earlier around the building and they had used it for a special briefing area. The FBI had erected a ten-foot-high Cyclone fence around the wooden fence, fifty feet away, and had installed a electronic gate-locking device. The three witnesses were as much prisoners as James was until the court-martial was over with and their lives weren't in as much danger. "How are you guys doing today?"

Instantly the look on Spencer's face changed to a jovial, elfish grin. "Great! Shrink . . . what has the outside world brought us today?"

"Some magazines." Martin held out a *Time* magazine to Spencer. "You'll like this one."

The front cover of the large-circulation weekly bore Spencer's picture. He was smiling and his Medal of Honor hung around his neck. The picture was expertly touched up to emphasize even more his boyish good looks and fiery blue eyes.

"Cute, Spence—real cute!" David Woods leaned over Spencer's shoulder and looked down at the cover. He patted Spence's rear. "Cute ass, too!"

Spencer ignored the kidding and kept looking at the cover.

"You falling in love with yourself?" David reached over to take the magazine and Spencer pointed to a person in the crowd. "Mary!"

Spencer nodded. Mary was in the background, a little out of focus but recognizable.

"I can see that's going to be framed," Arnason said, joining the kidding.

"Yep." Spencer smiled.

"So! How are you guys doing?" The psychiatrist sat down at the end of the picnic table and tried opening a conversation.

"Good . . . What's going on over at the trial?" Arnason asked.

"So far, they've just approved the board: four officers and

three enlisted men. James's lawyers demanded that there be enlisted men on the board, and according to the *Manual for Courts-Martial*, he's entitled to that privilege."

"What does he think? Enlisted men are going to go *easier* on him?" Woods was getting angry.

"They feel that he has a better chance than with all officers." The psychiatrist looked over at Spencer and met a large smile followed by a slow wink. "I must say they did a decent job picking the enlisted board members; Sergeant Major Thomas is black, Master Sergeant Valdez is Mexican, and Sergeant First Class Colorado is an American Indian."

"I know him" Arnason looked at Spencer. "He's a fine recon man. Two tours in Vietnam."

"Which one?" Martin asked. He was playing the psychiatrist's game of asking questions that didn't seem to have much impact but normally ended up as very important.

"Colorado . . . he's a pure blood Cheyenne. He even practices the old Indian religion and worships the manitou. I can't see James's lawyers letting him stay on the board without challenging him. He is one hard-core soldier."

"He was the only one they *didn't* challenge." The psychiatrist glanced again at Spencer and received the same smile and slow wink. A flash of irritation gave away what the shrink was thinking and Spencer smiled even more.

"That's interesting." Arnason shook his head.

"When do you think we'll be called on the stand?" Woods was getting tired of waiting.

"Probably late this afternoon or early tomorrow morning. I think the first witness will be Major General Garibaldi."

"He's here?" Spencer spoke with the smile still glued to his face. He knew that it was getting to the psychiatrist.

"Do you have to smile constantly, Corporal Barnett?"

"I'm *happy*, well adjusted, and recently laid." Spencer wiggled his eyebrows.

Lieutenant Colonel Martin turned away from Spencer. He had failed to get to the soldier and he knew it, but that didn't change his assignment. He was supposed to monitor all the witnesses for signs of strain, but actually he was the one who was feeling the strain. The Army's colonels review board had just released its recommendation list for promotion to colonel and his name wasn't on it. He was sure that the lieutenant general had taken him off the promotion list because of Spencer Barnett, but he couldn't prove it.

"Look at that." Spencer drew their attention to the cicada that had just fallen out of the pine tree they were sitting under.

"What is it?" The psychiatrist was city-bred.

"A cicada."

"Shit" Woods slipped over the seat away from the thrashing cicada. "Look at the size of that mother!"

A wasp dropped down out of the tree on her three-inch wings and grabbed the paralyzed cicada. The insect was too heavy for the giant wasp to fly away with, so the mother hunter used her legs to drag the cicada over the loose sand and her wings to give her a little lift. She walked her prey over to the trunk of the pine tree and climbed up the bark until she was about five feet off the ground before she let go and flew over the picnic table on her flight back to the communal nest that she shared with two of her sisters.

"Damn!" Woods leaned back as the giant wasp flew within a meter of his head.

"She won't bother you. She's too busy getting food for her larvae." Spencer sipped his warm Coke.

"That was one *big* fucking wasp!" Woods shook his head. "That thing could knock down a Cobra gunship!"

"Not quite, David." Spencer huffed and smiled over at the psychiatrist.

"So do we have to remain in uniform the rest of the day?" Arnason asked. He wanted to slip into shorts and get a little sun.

"No, but have your uniforms ready just in case they call you to appear." The psychiatrist glanced again at Spencer. "As soon as General Garibaldi is finished over in the court room, I want to bring him over here to brief you on what's going on so that there won't be any surprises when you testify."

"Fine with me. I want to see the colonel again." Spencer leaned over to untie his dress shoes. The sun was so hot that the spit shine was melting. He would have to polish them again as soon as it got dark, and then he would put them in the empty refrigerator in the back of the barracks so that the wax would harden.

"He's a *major general* now. . . ." The psychiatrist was becoming irritated with Spencer's constant referral to the Air Force general as a colonel.

"I know that." Spencer pulled off his socks and picked up his shoes. He started walking back to the barracks.

"We should be here by four."

Spencer nodded and disappeared into the dark barracks. He slipped out of his khaki pants and folded them neatly on a hanger before going back outside carrying an olive-drab Army blanket to lie on in the sun. He was wearing only his white briefs as he passed the psychiatrist.

"I hope you're going to have more than that on when the general comes over here."

"I might . . . sir." Spencer smiled and winked.

He lay on his back in the hot sun and felt the sweat forming pools in the eight-pack of muscles that covered his stomach. Woods was stretched out on a blanket a few feet away from him, wearing only his underwear too; neither of them had thought to bring shorts with them to the court-martial. Sergeant Arnason wore a pair of cut-off tiger pants that he always took with him to use as pajamas. Woods was sleeping on his stomach with one of his legs pulled up. Arnason tried reading the paperback book he held in front of him but the position was becoming very uncomfortable. He had to hold the book away from his body so that the sweat wouldn't ruin the pages. The upper right-hand corners of the pages were damp from his fingers turning them.

"Shit!" Arnason swore under his breath. A large drop of sweat fell off his nose and landed on the center of the page. "Christ, is it hot out here!" He adjusted his position on his blanket and decided to call it a day and go inside to take a shower.

Spencer moaned in his sleep.

Arnason stopped folding his blanket and looked over at the soldier.

Spencer moaned again but this time there was fear and pain in his voice.

Arnason laid his blanket down on the picnic table and sat on the bench. He used the back of his hand to wipe the sweat off his face and snapped it, sending a line of wet dots across the sandy soil.

Spencer started breathing very shallowly and rapidly in his deep sleep. He arched his back and whimpered.

Arnason started looking worried.

Spencer spoke. "Please? . . . Please . . . get the fuck away from me." He brought his legs up to his chest and curled into a fetal position on the warm blanket. "Colonel! That bitch is sticking her tongue out at me!" There was a pause, then Spencer mumbled under his breath, "Uh . . . huh . . . I will, Colonel." He sighed deeply like a person who was about to give up. "Oh . . . shit . . . her head is only a foot away from me! Colonel . . . I can't take this shit anymore!"

Spencer jerked upright on the blanket with his eyes wide open, scaring Arnason.

"Fuck it! Do you hear me, Sweet Bitch! Fuck *it* . . . fuck *you* . . . fuck *James!* . . . Fuck all your commie asses with elephant dicks!" Spencer's eyes weren't focused.

Arnason saw Woods staring at Spencer with a look of fear on his face. "Sarge . . . is he all right?"

Arnason nodded. "Shhh . . ."

Spencer dropped back down on the blanket and groaned again, then screamed at the top of his lungs. His own voice woke him up and he lay there blinking his eyes, drenched in sweat. He sucked in a lungful of air and shivered when he exhaled. "Fuck!"

"Bad dream?" Arnason spoke softly.

"Yeah." Spencer held his head in his hands and looked down between his legs as he sat on the blanket. "Real bad."

"Who's Sweet Bitch?" Arnason maintained the same tone of voice.

"She was the NVA lieutenant who ran our POW camp. . . . She used to really smoke my ass."

"How?" Arnason realized that Spencer had never before told anyone about what had happened in the POW camp.

"I was just dreaming about it." Spencer remained sitting on the blanket with his eyes locked on the large black letters printed on the cloth: USA. "She had captured a huge fucking snake . . . I mean *huge*." He looked at Arnason, who could see that Spencer's face was white. "It was bigger around than my waist and at least thirty feet long! Colonel Garibaldi said probably thirty-five feet!"

"She put you *in* the cage with it?"

"Yeah."

Woods felt like he was going to cry but fought the urge. Spencer wouldn't have been captured if Woods had insisted on staying back as the rear guard on the mission, instead of Spence.

Spencer continued, "They put a South Vietnamese officer in the cage the first night. . . . He committed suicide before dawn by hanging himself with his pants." Spencer's eyes lost their focus for a couple of seconds and he tried smiling but failed. "So, when they put me in the cage they stripped me naked. . . . I didn't give a fuck at first, but then when I saw Mother Kaa *close up*, even a pair of pants and a shirt would have helped . . . but being *naked*, I felt so . . . helpless." Spencer's hand started shaking. "She was one *big* snake."

"So what happened?" Arnason wanted to get Spencer's mind away from the snake.

"A Montagnard boy was hiding under the cage and shoved some bamboo sticks up through the floor in front of me so Mother Kaa couldn't touch me. . . . There was some kind of stuff rubbed on the bamboo, because she wouldn't come near it."

"Was the Montagnard boy the same one they killed?" David entered the conversation.

"Yes! How did you know that?" Spencer's eyes focused completely now and he joined his friends back at Camp McCall.

"We just came back from a mission over there with his father." Woods could see that Spencer was very interested and continued, "The old chief and his son have started a private war with the NVA and we set up a resupply for them."

Arnason shook his head. "We've been fools! We should have told you earlier about this!"

"Go on!" Spencer used his hands to emphasize.

"There's not a lot more to it. We set up a resupply drop and the Montagnards now have some modern weapons to fight with." David went over and took a seat near Arnason in the shade in front of the fan. "The Montagnards have a way of letting the NVA know that it's them killing their comrades."

"How's that?"

Arnason grabbed David's arm and shook his head.

"Tell me!" Spencer's jaws tightened.

"You don't need to know."

"Tell me!"

"They impale the NVA on bamboo stakes." Arnason watched for Spencer's reaction.

"Through their asses?"

"Yes . . ." Arnason's voice was a whisper.

"Good! Those mother fuckers deserve it!" Spencer smiled, "Payback is a bitch!"

Arnason sighed. He was worried that talking about it would break Spencer, but the opposite had happened. Spencer actually looked relieved of a great guilt.

"They put that little Montagnard boy on one of those stakes and made me watch. . . ."

"That's not the way the chief tells the story."

"What did he say?"

"He said that you volunteered to take the boy's place."

Spencer shrugged.

"That was a brave thing to do, Spence. . . ." Arnason nodded.

"No . . . actually it was the cowardly thing to do. The brave thing would have been to sit there and *watch* them torture that kid and do nothing." Spencer's logic was clear to his teammates.

"Why did they bury the boy underneath you?" David risked asking for an answer to the question that had been bothering him ever since they had rescued Spencer and he had seen the tiny hand in the dirt under his teammate.

"They had left him on the stake for three days in the jungle heat . . ." Spencer didn't have to go into detail for his teammates—they knew what a body looked like after three days in the sun, "and they weren't going to bury him. He was being made an example for the rest of the Montagnards because he had helped me." Spencer grinned and added, "I bet they wish now that they had left that kid alone!"

"So who buried him?"

"I did, and then James came up with the bright idea that I should be buried up to my neck in the grave *over* the kid. . . . He thought that was funny."

"James did that?" Arnason felt his throat muscles tighten in anger.

"Yeah, and then he was going to blow my brains out, but only after I suffered for a couple of days in the sun. Nice guy, huh?"

"I didn't know. . . ." David felt the first tear coming.

"Don't start bawling on me, Woods!" Spencer frowned.

Woods smiled. "You are one hard-core southern boy!"

"That's right! I owe you! . . . Remember?" Spencer sprung at Woods and knocked him off the blanket onto the sandy ground.

"Get off me!" Woods used his leg to flip Spencer over on his back and jumped up on his feet. "Or I'll have to really whip your skinny ass good!" David dropped down into a wrestler's crouch.

"Remember back in the hotel? You called me a boy in front of Mary . . . remember?"

"Yep . . . *boy* . . . I remember." David braced himself for the attack that followed.

Arnason rose and began heading toward the barracks to take a cold shower. It was too hot even to watch them.

"You'd better stay here and save this Nebraska punk from a sure death!" Spencer spoke from his position on the bottom as he tried bucking to keep his shoulders from being pinned.

"Kill yourselves . . . you'll dehydrate first!" Arnason came back and changed the direction of the fan so that it blew over the two men wrestling. He didn't know how much good it would do either of them, but at least he had done something thoughtful.

Spencer lay flat on his back, looking up at the cloudless blue Carolina sky. Woods lay on his stomach a few feet away, spitting out the sand that had gotten into his mouth.

"Shit . . . I'm going to die!" Spencer spoke at the sky.

Woods gagged, struggled to his feet, and lunged toward an outside hose for some water. Spencer had been raised in the

South and could almost predict what was going to happen next. He rose on one elbow and started laughing as Woods turned on the faucet and held the end of the hose up over his head. The first rush of water was *hot*.

"Oh fuck!" David dropped the hose in the sand and tried brushing the hot water off his matted-down hair.

"Use the hose now, you dumb ass." Spencer roared with laughter at the stupidity of his northern-born teammate; everybody down South knew that the sun baked the water trapped in a rubber hose. "It's cold now after you used up all the *hot* water!"

"Spence, you *knew* that was going to happen!" David picked up the rubber hose and wet himself down. The water felt great after wrestling in the rough sand. "Shit, I've got sand burns all over me!"

"Baby!" Spencer could feel his skin burning from the same thing.

"What's going on back here?" The familiar voice caught Spencer's ear.

"Colonel!" Spencer jumped up from the ground and rushed over to shake hands with the Air Force major general.

"Don't you dare, Spencer Barnett!" The general pushed the soldier's hand away and hugged him.

The general's aide-de-camp was a couple of feet behind the old fighter pilot, followed closely by the psychiatrist, who tried shoving his way around the aide so that he could see the reunion between the two POWs.

"I brought you something." Garibaldi waved for his aide to bring forward the large box that was being carried by his driver.

Spencer smiled the instant he saw what the driver was carrying. "Colonel! Damn, you do keep your word."

The driver set the case of Del Monte fruit cocktail down on the picnic table.

"I don't understand." The psychiatrist looked puzzled.

"I promised . . ." The general began to explain, then decided that it would be better if it remained between him and Spencer. "It's a *private* joke."

"So how have you been, Colonel?" Spencer patted the general on his shoulder. The aide smiled. He had been briefed by the general about Spencer.

"Fine, just fine, Spencer... but you don't look so good right now... and who's your friend?"

Woods stepped forward shyly, wearing only his wet underwear in front of the senior officer. He held out his hand and tried smiling. "I'm Sergeant Woods, sir. I was with the team that..."

"Damn Sam! I'm sorry! I didn't recognize you without... all of your make-up on!"

"That's *camouflage* paint... Colonel!" Spencer corrected the Air Force general. "Anyone who flies Piper Cubs should know the difference."

"Well, excuse me... Spencer!" The general sat down on the edge of the picnic table. "If you have something cold to drink, we'll wait out here until you two shower and get some clothes on and then we have to talk some business."

"We can handle that, Colonel." Spencer waved for the aide to follow them inside the barracks and showed him where the food refrigerator was against the back wall.

The psychiatrist waited until the aide and driver had departed before asking the general the question that was burning on his tongue: "Well? How do you feel?"

"Not as good as I had hoped for and not as bad as I had feared." The general kept his eyes glued on the open doorway where Spencer had disappeared. He could hear the showers running in the building.

"What do you think of Corporal Barnett?"

"He looks good! I can't believe he's filled out so much!" The general was amazed at how fast Spencer had gained back his body weight. "Of course, he's only a kid... seventeen years old."

"Do you think he'll crack in the courtroom?"

"No... he's a tough young man."

"Are you *sure*, General?"

Major General Garibaldi turned slightly on the picnic table and stared hard at the psychiatrist. "You know, you might have some book-smarts, but you sure don't know *people*. That boy in there kept *me* alive when I was ready to quit! He went through some torture that I *know* I couldn't have withstood. . . . Yes, Dr. Martin, I'm *quite* sure he can handle a courtroom drama."

"I didn't mean to be rude, General."

"You never do, Doctor, but you always are." Garibaldi saw his aide returning carrying two Mountain Dew sodas. "We'd better change the topic, but rest assured that Spencer won't let us down. I think after the initial shock of seeing James wears off, he'll be fantastic. We have to be ready for that first encounter, though."

"Do you think we should give Corporal Barnett some Valium before he appears before the court-martial?"

"You really don't know your patients, do you?" Garibaldi shook his head. "Don't be here when Spencer returns."

"It's my job, General!" Martin's professional competence was being challenged.

"Not anymore. Spencer doesn't even take aspirin, let alone a depressant and mind-controlling drug!" Garibaldi waved the psychiatrist away. "I tolerated your bullshit because you were supposed to be the best psychiatrist in the Army . . . but obviously that decision was based on your grade point average and not your common sense!"

The psychiatrist left, boiling mad and blaming Spencer for his failure.

Major General Garibaldi sat under the loblolly pines and thought about his session in the courtroom. He had feared a personal attack from James's lawyers, and when it had come he was surprised that it was based on James's charges that *he* had also collaborated with the enemy and therefore was not qualified to testify against him. That had been easy to defend against; the hardest part had been looking at James sitting so near to him with that arrogant grin plastered on his face.

"Where did our *friend* go?" Spencer stepped through the doorway. "I saw him leaving."

"He's got some business elsewhere." Garibaldi smiled. It was good seeing the young warrior again. "I didn't have a chance to make it to your awards ceremony. . . . You know that I would have given anything to be there."

"Sure . . . I understand, Colonel."

"I've been given command of an important F-16 fighter

unit and we were conducting something very secret at the time."

"You don't need to explain yourself to me, Colonel." Spencer curled his mouth in a wide grin.

"True, I knew you'd understand. Now, about our *buddy* in there." Garibaldi nodded toward the building that had been modified for the court-martial. "They're going to bring you in the first thing tomorrow morning. The defense lawyers wanted to bring you in later this afternoon but the law officer ruled that it would be in the best interest of the court that you appear in the morning." Garibaldi saw the puzzled look on Spencer's face. "They figure that you'll be tired and easy to break after having to wait around all day wondering what's going on inside."

"It doesn't make a difference to me."

"I know." Garibaldi finished his Mountain Dew and set the can down on the wooden tabletop. "I'll be sitting in the back of the courtroom if you need a friendly face to look at."

"Thanks, Colonel."

"No problem." Garibaldi felt his throat begin to tighten up and quickly added before he lost the ability to talk, "Spencer . . . *thanks*."

Spencer smiled his wide, heart-winning grin. "You're welcome . . . anytime, Colonel."

The gray-haired general just nodded. A lot of emotion and understanding had been passed between the two warriors in just a few words.

The Army trial counsel had made sure that Corporal Barnett and the other witnesses he planned on using for the morning session were in the courtroom a couple of hours before the trial was due to start. The tactic was an excellent one on the part of Brigadier General Heller. He knew that one of the best ways to break a witness was to catch him disoriented in unfamiliar surroundings. The extra time in the courtroom setting would give his witnesses time to relax and prepare themselves mentally for the arrival of Specialist James and his defense counsel, Brigadier General Tallon, and his dozen assistant lawyers from the civilian sector.

General Heller sat across the table from Spencer and played

with a triangular piece of toast in the yoke of a partially eaten egg. "Let's review it one more time."

Spencer nodded in agreement and kept eating.

"The tactics that General Tallon will use aren't going to be very nice. Their only hope is to get you to lose your temper or even break you on the witness stand so that they can rule you mentally incompetent as a witness. They tried that yesterday on General Garibaldi and it backfired on them; that's why they've recalled him as a witness this morning, along with the trick they tried pulling yesterday."

Spencer swallowed a mouthful of chipped beef on toast. "What trick, sir?"

"They want you to testify late in the day so that you'll be tired and nervous after having to watch and wait all day." Heller sipped his orange juice. "I think that's why they called for General Garibaldi to return to the witness stand this morning."

"Fine. It isn't going to bother me at all."

"Are you sure?" Heller was secretly worried. Lieutenant Colonel Martin had briefed him on Barnett's mental condition and refusal to cooperate.

"Tell me what to do, General, and I'll do it." Spencer smiled over his fork.

"Great!" Heller leaned back in his chair and looked at his watch. "We've got twenty minutes to have these breakfast trays taken back to the mess hall."

Sergeants Arnason and Woods stacked the trays and handed them to the guards. Arnason looked at Spencer and saw that the star witness was relaxed. General Heller was a very smart military lawyer, having them eat breakfast in the courtroom. It made them all feel like they were now in their own homes, instead of a mysterious courtroom.

Woods lit a cigarette in the hallway outside the courtroom and blew the first lungful of blue smoke against the row of windows. "Do you think they've got enough guards around this place?"

Arnason answered, "You're just seeing the MP detachment. . . . There are two battalions of infantry circling Camp McCall from the Eighty-second Airborne Division and nine Special Forces A-teams deployed in the swamps and along the streams and rivers within five miles of here."

"I feel like *I'm* the prisoner instead of James." Spencer put his head against one of the windows and looked up at the light blue sky. It was still very humid and hot outside, but the Army had installed a huge air-conditioning system in the courtroom building almost overnight. "Here come the press."

Woods blew another lungful of smoke against the windows. "Fucking commies . . . The KGB couldn't have better friends during this fucking war."

"Be nice now, Woods!" Arnason's voice was mocking. "Remember the First Amendment rights of the press."

"I've never read that they have the right to push wounded men off helicopters so that they could fly along and get pictures for their damn magazines!" Everyone standing in the group knew what Woods was referring to. During the battle of the Ia Drang Valley, a reporter-photographer had shoved two walking wounded out of a helicopter so that he could fly back to the hospital and photograph the arrival of wounded American soldiers from the *soldiers' perspective*. One of the men he had shoved off the Medevac had died shortly thereafter from shock; and the photographer had won an award for the *realistic* series of photographs, complete with blood covering the bed of the chopper.

"We'd better get back inside the courtroom and take our seats." Arnason nodded in the direction of the stained double doors.

"I've got to take a shit first." Spencer patted his stomach. "I ate too much."

"I'll go with you." After what had happened at the cabin, Woods and Arnason had decided on their own that they wouldn't leave Spencer alone until the court-martial was over.

The door to the latrine swung open and then slammed shut. Spencer and Woods could hear the water get turned on in one of the sinks and someone using one of the urinals.

"I can't believe that damn Heller! The nerve of that bastard!"

"Take it easy, General. . . . He's a smart son of a bitch—we knew that all along." The second voice was a deep bass.

"I can't believe he brought that little bastard here already and they had *breakfast* in the courtroom!"

"Smart . . . if you ask me," the bass voice echoed in the large latrine.

"You know that screws up our game plan." The urinal was flushed by the unseen man and a second faucet was turned on.

"A little, but we shouldn't have a problem breaking him. The psychiatrist's report stated that he was very unstable and prone to violent temper tantrums." The bass voice sounded very confident.

"You've got a point there. That's all we'll have to do is bait him a little."

"Bingo, General."

Spencer had heard enough. He flushed the commode and stepped out of the booth. Woods hurried to fasten his pants. Spencer walked over to a sink near the brigadier general and a black man dressed in a very expensive suit. The black man had his suit coat off and was washing his face and hands. The general glanced at Spencer, not quite sure what to make of him and not recognizing who he was.

"David . . . do you think we'll be here long this morning?"

Woods didn't know what to make of Spencer's comment and answered, "I don't think we'll be here past noon. Why, Spence?"

The looks on both the general's and the black lawyer's faces were identical—pure shock.

"I guess I can last that long without having a temper tantrum." Spencer hid his smile by splashing water over his face.

Woods understood what Spencer was doing. "I *hope* so, Spence. You haven't had one in a couple of weeks . . . at least."

"Yeah. We'd better check in with General Heller before the trial starts." Spencer dried his face with a paper towel and looked over at the general, whose face was a bright red. "Morning, sir!"

Woods left the latrine a step behind Spencer. He waited until they were down the hall a couple of meters before starting to laugh. "Damn! We just ruined their day!"

"Whose day?" General Heller stepped out of the courtroom,

holding the door open with one hand. "Where have you two been?"

Woods told the general what had happened and the horse laugh from the brigadier general carried down the hallway and through the latrine door to his peer.

As soon as Spencer entered the courtroom, flashbulbs started popping. He was escorted to the front-row seats behind the trial counsel's table and given a seat next to Sergeants Arnason and Woods. The chair on Spencer's other side was marked with a piece of white tape labeled: MAJOR GENERAL GARIBALDI.

The doors behind Spencer opened and the reporters turned and began jockeying for position and taking photographs. Spencer didn't need to be told that James had arrived.

Specialist Fourth Class Mohammed James had been very well rehearsed by his lawyers. As he walked down the aisle he smiled and nodded at friendly faces in the crowd of reporters, especially those he recognized from his interviews with reporters from the black periodicals. He knew that he was fighting for his life and that the evidence against him was very strong. James approached the back of Spencer's seat and paused. The courtroom became quiet as everyone watched what was going to happen between James and the star witness for the prosecution.

"It's good seeing you again, Barnett." James's voice was even and carried a familiar tone. "I'm glad that you've recovered from the POW camp."

Spencer smiled before he rose and turned around. General Heller held his breath.

"It's good to be back in the States, isn't it." James made the question a statement.

"*Very* good." Spencer kept the smile on his face as the flashbulbs reflected off his sparkling, fiery blue eyes.

"No hard feelings?" James held out his hand.

"I can't shake hands with you, James . . . but I will say that I won't lie . . . the *truth* will be enough." Spencer sat back down before the MPs could move James over to the defense table.

Brigadier General Tallon leaned over and whispered in

James's ear, "That was a very *dumb* move! Don't you ever pull that shit on me again and take me by surprise!"

James glanced over at his black lawyer, who had been hired by the mosque out of Detroit. The lawyer shook his head in agreement with the general.

A side door to the courtroom opened and the seven members of the general court-martial board walked in and took their seats behind the long table that faced the rows of chairs.

Major General Koch took his time looking around the courtroom before making a very short opening statement: "Gentlemen, the general court-martial proceedings of Specialist Mohammed James are now in session. Defense counsel, I believe the floor is yours and you may recall your witness."

Brigadier General Tallon stood and adjusted his black leather general's belt on his short-sleeved khaki uniform before calling Major General Garibaldi to the witness stand.

The double doors opened and the Air Force general strode into the room and went directly to the witness chair that had been placed at the left front corner of the long conference table the board sat behind.

"General, the oath that you took yesterday still applies in this courtroom today." General Koch spoke to his peer in a controlled, professional tone of voice. He did not like the idea of a general being grilled in front of the press, but Garibaldi was a prime witness.

"General Garibaldi . . . you testified yesterday that you found a picture of the defendant beating another prisoner while both of them were prisoners of war."

"That's true. I was being interrogated by Lieutenant Van Pao, the camp commander and NVA intelligence officer. The Polaroid snapshot was lying under the edge of her desk."

"And you just reached down and picked it up?" Tallon was attacking. "And did you slip it into your pocket?"

"No."

"What did you do, General?"

"I tipped over a box of sundry candy, and while I was picking up the individual packages of Chuckles—"

"Chuckles?" Tallon interrupted.

"Yes . . . Chuckles. They're a jellied candy."

"North Vietnamese?"

"No, American."

"What were the North Vietnamese . . . in Laos . . . doing with *boxes* of American candy?"

"Ask Specialist James where they got them. . . . He helped them."

"Please . . . I would like that statement struck from the record." Tallon addressed the president of the board.

"Please strike General Garibaldi's last statement from the record." Koch glanced over at Colonel Chan, the law officer for the general court-martial, and received a confirming nod.

"Do you know where the North Vietnamese got American candy from, General Garibaldi?" Tallon asked with a smile.

"No, but I assume they got the sundry packages through the black market in South Vietnam."

"You *assume*."

"Yes."

"And why was the *North Vietnamese* commander giving you candy . . . candy by the *box?*"

"She felt like it."

"For no reason?"

"I don't know her reason."

"Did she do it as a *reward* for service rendered?"

Major General Garibaldi smiled at the one-star general before answering him. "General, when you are a prisoner of war for over a year . . . in many cases even less time . . . and someone—*anyone*—offers you food and especially fruit or sugar, you'll take it without asking why."

"You are assuming that I would?"

"Yes . . . before they tortured you . . . in *your* case."

General Koch intervened. "Gentlemen! Please! You're in a courtroom and I shouldn't have to remind you of that!"

"So . . . General . . . what did you do with the photograph once you had *found* it just lying there in front of you on the floor?"

"I snuck it out of the office and gave it to the Montagnard boy who came to empty our night pots and asked him to take it to the Special Forces men at A Shau."

"Do you speak the Montagnard language?"

"No."

"Then how did you communicate with a *child* well enough to tell him to walk twenty miles to an American base camp?"

"Sign language and a drawing in the dirt."

"You must be very good at drawing."

"I was motivated."

Tallon backed off a little. He was being outmaneuvered by the general. "What is a 'night pot,' General?"

"A clay pot that was placed in the POWs' cages and used for body functions."

"And this little boy came every day to empty them?"

"Yes."

"How old was the boy?"

"Between eight and ten. It's hard to tell exactly with the Montagnards because they are a small-framed people."

"And what you are trying to tell the court is that a *tiny* eight-year-old boy took the photograph and by *himself* went all that way through the jungle to deliver this picture"—Tallon held up the photograph for the press to see—"to a Special Forced A-camp twenty miles away?" Tallon walked over to where Garibaldi sat and waved the Polaroid shot in front of his face. "Do you *expect* us to believe that?"

"Yes."

"Isn't the *true* story that you collaborated with the enemy?" Tallon paused, waiting for Garibaldi to lose his temper over the accusation, and when he saw that it wasn't having the effect he had wished for, he added, "Isn't the truth that you agreed to help frame Specialist James by having the picture sent to the American camp and your payment was the box of highly desired candy?"

"No."

"Isn't it true that Specialist James underwent extreme torture at the hands of the enemy and had refused to compromise his high standards and that you and Corporal Barnett *schemed* to have James charged with treason and murder?"

"No." Garibaldi's voice remained extremely calm.

"Isn't it true that the Montagnard boy *worked* for the NVA?"

"No."

"I thought you said that the boy carried your night pots."

"That's true."

"Then he *worked* for the NVA!"

"No . . . he worked to stay *alive*." Garibaldi turned his head so that he could look directly into Tallon's eyes. "There *is* a difference, you know."

"Working carrying night pots or photographs is basically the same." Tallon felt that he had pressed that issue enough and had made the point he wanted to make, so he changed the subject. "Now tell me, General . . . you testified yesterday that Specialist James struck you."

"Yes."

"Where?"

"Across the side of my face."

"When?"

"When *he* escorted Corporal Barnett and me down to the river to bathe."

"He escorted you?"

"Yes."

"Alone?"

"No."

"Who else was there?"

"Two NVA soldiers."

"Then *they* escorted all *three* of you POWs."

"You can say that if you like, but Specialist James was carrying an AK-47 assault rifle."

Reporters in the back of the room started laughing. Sergeants Arnason and Woods smiled over the witty remark. Spencer stared hard at the defense counsel, causing the man to blush when he looked over at him.

"It could have been *empty* and was being used as a decoy to divide you three POWs and conquer."

"It could have."

"Then you agree that it would be *possible* for the NVA to make it *look* like Specialist James was a traitor."

"Yes."

"Good! Then couldn't it have been an NVA tactic to force James to brag in front of you about killing Americans and becoming an NVA general, as you testified yesterday?"

"It could have, but—"

"No buts, General! It could have happened!" Tallon spun

around and looked at Brigadier General Heller and his trial team. "Your witness, counsel!"

"I have no questions at this time." Heller nodded at Tallon.

"Present your next witness, please." Koch spoke to Heller.

"I'd like Sergeant David Woods to take the stand, please."

Woods looked over at Arnason. They had expected Spencer to be the next one called. David swore in and took his seat in front of the rows of reporters.

"Sergeant Woods, would you please tell the board what happened during your visit to the Twenty-fourth Corps Headquarters in Vietnam." Heller nodded for David to begin.

"Yes sir. I was leaving the snackbar in the headquarters building when I thought I saw James walking down the hall wearing a captain's uniform and carrying a briefcase. I called out to him and he stopped walking and turned around with a very scared look on his face."

"What did you do then?"

"I started walking toward him."

"And what did he do?"

"He ran out of the building and disappeared. I followed him outside but he was gone."

"Members of the board, I would like to submit as evidence exhibits A, B, H, and K. They are all statements taken under oath from officers and enlisted men at the Twenty-fourth Corps Headquarters who have *positively* identified Specialist James as the person who posed as a captain in the United States Army and was seen at the Twenty-fourth Corps Headquarters tracing battle overlays during a period when he was reported as being a prisoner of war in Laos and under enemy control!" General Heller looked at Tallon. "Your witness, counsel!"

Tallon leaned over and listened to the black lawyer from Detroit whisper in his ear before he approached Woods at the witness stand. "Tell me, Sergeant Woods . . . how far away from you was this person who you claim was Specialist James?"

"Ten feet."

"Did he have his back to you?"

"Yes, until I called his name . . . James!"

"Please, just answer yes or no." Tallon was trying to intimidate the young soldier. "Do you understand the seriousness of the charges against Specialist James?"

"Yes."

"Do you hate black soldiers?"

"No."

"Just a little?"

"No."

"Then you are *totally not* prejudiced?"

"No."

"You *are* prejudiced?"

"No."

"What are you?"

Woods paused for a long time and then said, "I can't answer that question yes or no, General."

Tallon smiled. The young sergeant wasn't going to be easy. "Tell me, Sergeant, how well do you know Specialist James?"

"We went to Recondo School together. I know him pretty well." Woods glanced over at James sitting behind his table, next to his civilian lawyers.

"Well enough to be able to recognize him from the back?"

"I'm a recon man, sir . . . I can do that in the *dark*."

"Really? Aren't you bragging just a little bit?"

"Nope . . . as long as I have enough light to see a little."

"Fine. Let's see just how good you are." Tallon looked over at General Koch. "Sir, I would like to conduct an experiment."

"As long as you keep it inside the courtroom, counselor." General Koch looked again at Colonel Chan for a legal opinion and received a nod in agreement that the procedure was proper.

"Thank you. We will." Tallon beckoned one of the guards to come over to his defense table. "Would you escort Sergeant Woods outside for a minute please and wait until I call for him to come back inside. Thank you."

Woods and the MP went out into the hallway. David lit a cigarette and stared out the window, wondering what the defense counsel was up to. The door opened a few minutes later and Tallon called them back inside. The courtroom lights had been turned off and only a faint light glimmered in a projection booth high up on the back wall, throwing off just enough light to cast dark shadows in the room but not enough light to see anything except the outlines of a dozen men standing in a row next to the wall at the far end of the room.

"Now, Sergeant Woods . . . is there enough light?" Tallon's voice was extremely cocky.

"Give me a second for my eyes to adjust."

"Sure, take all the time you need."

David waited until his eyes were accustomed to the light and looked around the room before telling Tallon that he was ready. He had located the row of board members and Arnason and Spencer sitting in the front row of the audience.

"Can you see the row of men standing next to the opposite wall?" Tallon's voice almost broke out in a mocking laugh.

"Yes sir."

"How far away do you think they are?"

Woods located himself in the room and made the easy judgment call from having seen the room lit up before. "Thirty-five feet."

"And you said that Specialist James was ten feet away from you and had his back to you, right?"

"Yes . . . in a lit hallway."

"Right, Sergeant . . . but you said that you could identify him in the dark."

David had used the time to examine each of the men's silhouettes while the defense counsel talked. He was sure that James wasn't standing against the wall. He was being tricked. Woods glanced back over to where Arnason sat and noticed that his arm lay along the back of the chair. Arnason saw the angle of Woods's head and guessed that he was looking over at him, and he pointed with his whole hand up to the back row. Woods saw James's head and shoulders silhouetted against the wood paneling. Tallon had screwed up. If the counsel had sat him down a couple of rows, James would have blended in with the massed crowd.

"Well, Sergeant, have you located Specialist James in that row of men?"

"No sir."

"Then you *can't* identify him in the dark as you said you could."

"I didn't say that, General. I said that I couldn't locate him in that row of men against the wall. He's not there . . . he's sitting up there in the spectator stands."

The lights came back on and flashbulbs hurt everybody's eyes as the news people took pictures of the soldier who could see in the dark.

"Thank you, Sergeant." Tallon's voice was curt. "Your witness, counsel!"

General Heller stood up smiling. "I have no further questions, sir," he said to the president of the board.

The rest of the morning the lawyers called on witnesses for and against Specialist James, with most of the witnesses for him coming from the membership of the Brotherhood and the Detroit mosque. The trial counsel tried sticking to the charges against James, while the defense tried lining up character witnesses who praised James's childhood.

Right before it was time to break for lunch, Brigadier General Tallon called for Corporal Barnett to appear on the witness stand. The courtroom was stunned by the cheap tactic. Spencer smiled and swore in before the president of the board. He had been waiting for anything to happen and wasn't shocked or caught off guard, as the media was, by Tallon's waiting until everyone was tired and hungry before calling the star witness.

"I know you have been called here by the trial counsel, but I feel that you also are a prime witness for the defense. You were a prisoner with Specialist James, and if I'm not mistaken, you were captured by the North Vietnamese during the same battle." Tallon looked at Spencer, who just looked back at him.

"Well? Were you?"

"What?"

"Captured during the same battle with James?"

"Yes."

"Were you *both* beaten by the NVA soldiers?"

"No."

"Specialist James has testified already that he was beaten by the NVA when he was captured. Are you calling him a liar?"

"Yes."

A buzz filled the courtroom from whispered conversation in the press booth.

"I see." Tallon went back over to the defense table and conversed with the other lawyers and with James. He approached Spencer again smiling. "Do you remember any photographs being taken while you were being tortured?"

"No . . . I was preoccupied." The tiny little smile attached to the corner of Spencer's mouth brought roars of laughter from the spectators and forced the president to use his gavel to regain order in the courtroom

"Then you never saw anyone take any photographs?"

"I already said no."

"Don't get cocky, Corporal!"

Spencer stared at the brigadier general while the trial counsel appealed the treatment of the witness.

"All right, I withdraw my last remark." Tallon was regrouping—nothing was going right for him. "Did Specialist James take part . . . any part . . . in torturing you while you were a POW?"

"Yes."

"Are you *sure* that he did it of his own free will?"

"Yes."

"How can you be so sure?"

"Look at his face in the picture. Is that an expression of a man who is being *forced* to beat another prisoner or the face of a man *enjoying* what he's doing?"

"I'll ask the damn questions, soldier!"

Major General Koch beat the desktop with his gavel to regain control. "Gentlemen! Please . . . I must have order. Corporal Barnett, please answer only the questions you are asked!"

"Yes sir."

"Now, Corporal Barnett . . . we all know that you are a decorated war hero. You even hold the Medal of Honor, our nation's highest award for valor. . . . Congratulations!" Tallon smiled. "Let me ask you a question, though: do you hate black people?"

"Most of them." Spencer didn't hesitate.

"Do you hate Specialist James?"

"Yes."

The courtroom became a tomb of quiet.

"Well, if you hate black people, just because they're black . . . and you hate Specialist James, who's very black . . . how do we know that you're not lying about him beating you?"

Spencer sat quietly in his chair. Brigadier General Heller felt his heart beating faster. Slowly Spencer leaned over and untied his shoes. He slipped off his socks and held his feet up so that the members of the board could see the soles of his feet. The scar tissue could be seen from across the room. He held his feet up for a full minute and then stood up and unbuttoned his shirt and laid it over the back of his chair, followed by his T-shirt. The crisscrossed pattern of the scars made good material for the photographers' cameras.

"If you want me to drop my pants, I'll show you the scars from the bamboo rod James used to whip me with when I was tied to a bamboo pole." Spencer's voice carried no malice, just fact.

Tallon's breath caught in his throat as he stood looking at the handsome soldier's scarred body. He was James's defense attorney, but he also was an Army officer and a human being.

Spencer saw the look in Tallon's eyes and added, "They don't hurt anymore, but they sure did when James and Sweet Bitch were putting them there."

The sound of the gavel striking the table filled the room. "This general court-martial is adjourned until two P.M." Major General Koch had seen enough and so had the board for one session. Everyone in the courtroom needed a break from the tension that was building up. Reporters raced from the building to make telephone calls back to their offices. They all sensed a big story brewing.

Brigadier General Tallon and all of James's lawyers sat around the large table in the mess hall. The conversation was grim.

"We are not going to win our case if we can't establish ourselves during the Articles 104 and 105—aiding the enemy and misconduct as a prisoner—portion of this court-martial. As far as I'm concerned, we already lost the Article 106 charges when they accepted those damn statements as evidence from those men who identified James dressed as an Army captain," said the Black Muslim lawyer.

"I agree, counselor, but the *critical* charges are coming up next—Article 118. . . . If they can make murder charges stick, James is going to jail for a very long time. He can survive the charges under Article 106 for spying and even all the rest because we can say that he broke under torture . . . but killing one's fellow American soldiers in combat is going to be impossible to appeal and plead mercy." Tallon looked over at the black lawyer and added, "Remember that there's a *death* penalty for murder in the military."

"There's a death penalty for spying and one for aiding the enemy." The deep voice of the civilian lawyer got even deeper.

"Yes, I know that, but like I said earlier, we can get around a death sentence on those charges because of the extreme pressure a POW is under. Nobody nowadays expects a prisoner of war to withstand extreme torture and not talk."

"It looks like that white corporal did. . . ." The black lawyer tried smiling but Tallon caught the hate in his voice and looked hard into the man's eyes.

"There are no witnesses to any murder that James is charged with, and all twenty-three counts are based on what James said to General Garibaldi and Barnett while he was a POW. . . . That won't count for a number of reasons, with the best one being that James can't testify against himself." Tallon didn't like the look in the black lawyer's eyes and he stopped talking to look at the rest of the black lawyers who had all come from the same black law firm in Detroit. There was something very wrong in the way they looked and acted, almost as if they were not Americans but representatives of a foreign country.

"Let's see how it goes this afternoon." The senior civilian lawyer pushed away his steel tray and stood up. "Personally, I think there is enough doubt to sway the board on the aiding-the-enemy charges, and we can always fall back onto severe brainwashing to get James to copy those overlays in the headquarters building. . . . Maximum would be a couple of years in a federal stockade."

"I agree. We do have a chance, and when you add in all the

racial unrest throughout the country . . . they just might drop the whole damn thing to hold down black rioting in the big cities." Tallon saw the sparkle in the senior lawyer's eyes. He had made that statement to see what the effect would be.

"You just might have a point there, General!" The lawyer looked over at his assistants. "That was very good food, considering it was Army chow."

"There have been a lot of *changes* in the military in recent years." Tallon was becoming very uneasy with the black lawyers.

"Not enough and too late." The comment almost was racial. The lawyers left the brigadier general sitting alone at the table.

Heller had been watching the conversation from his table on the other side of the room where they had sectioned off a portion of the mess hall for members of the trial team so that the two factions could talk openly during their lunch break.

"I think James is going to jail for a very long time." Arnason made the open comment to the small group of men crowded around one of the tables drinking coffee. General Heller had called all of them together after lunch to have a strategy session.

"Let's not bet on it. Remember what's going on *outside* Camp McCall. There's a lot of racial unrest and I wouldn't be surprised if the President himself didn't step forward and pardon James for anything he's charged with while he was a POW. . . . No, our *best* and surest charges are going to be under Article 118 . . . murder." Heller bit his bottom lip.

"I was on that patrol in Recondo School where Sergeant McDonald was sure James killed one of our guys under fire. . . . " Woods's voice sounded as if it was going to break.

"We've got your statement and Barnett's too, but that's all very weak circumstantial evidence." General Heller smiled. "I have a real surprise for James and his galley of lawyers this afternoon. . . . We might not make twenty-three charges of murder stick, but I think I can nail him for three of them."

"How?" Arnason leaned forward in his chair.

"A surprise!" Heller patted Spencer's shoulder. "You did real good in there this morning. I don't think I could have thought up a better response to Tallon's question about the beatings. I was looking at the board's faces when you pulled off your shirt and *all* of them were impressed, with maybe one exception."

"Who was that?" Arnason whispered the question as the defense team walked past them on their way back to the courtroom.

"Sergeant Colorado . . . the Indian." Heller rubbed his chin. "There's something wrong there, especially the way he stares at Corporal Barnett."

"I haven't noticed, but I will when we return this afternoon." Arnason had wondered why the defense hadn't challenged Sergeant Colorado when they had started the proceedings. Colorado had a reputation for being one hard-assed NCO.

The press area was already packed when the trial team entered the courtroom and Spencer was escorted back up to the witness stand.

"I don't have any further questions at this time, sir." Tallon knew that he had lost in his first attempt at breaking the star witness and was trying to recoup his losses.

Major General Koch looked over at Heller. "Do you have any questions for this witness?"

Heller stood up slowly and looked over at Tallon and the sea of black faces surrounding him. "Yes, I do, sir . . . quite a few."

Brigadier General Heller took his time asking Spencer questions about his short but emotionally destructive period of time as a POW. Spencer described in detail the incidents with the huge reticulated python and the impaling of the live Montagnard boy on the bamboo stake and his being forced to watch the execution from less than three feet away and his three days of being forced to sit in front of the sun-swelled corpse. Even the most left-wing reporter was moved by Spencer's story and more than one reporter flashed hate-filled looks over at James.

Spencer left the witness stand unchallenged by the defense and took his seat again behind the trial counsel's table. He took his time studying the faces of the members of the general court-martial board as each lawyer reviewed his position on the first set of charges and then on the second set. Twice Spencer caught Sergeant Colorado staring at him; the third time he turned his head and saw the senior NCO watching him, Spencer stared back. The exchange was very interesting. Spencer sensed that the Indian was looking for a crack in his armor. Spencer attacked: he smiled.

Sergeant First Class Colorado smiled back. He knew that Spencer was definitely from the warrior clan and would have made a perfect Cheyenne warrior, maybe even a war chief when he had lived a few more years, but that would be very unlikely in these modern times. Spencer Barnett wouldn't live another twenty-four hours. The Brotherhood had a lot of money and the small ranch Colorado had dreamed about for years had already been bought and paid for in his name.

Arnason saw the penetrating stares passing between the NCO and Barnett and couldn't figure out why Colorado was glaring at Spencer with a hunting look in his eyes. The two of them should be friends because they were so much alike. Arnason decided that he would risk introducing Colorado to Spencer after the afternoon session, even though there might be a bit of a risk in compromising the court-martial. He knew where the Indian would probably be right after it got dark out, but the problem would be getting either Spencer out of the secure compound or Colorado into it after dark. The FBI and the CIA were not taking *any* chances after Spencer's little escape to Arlington Cemetery with his foster brother. That escapade had embarrassed the Agency and it wouldn't happen twice.

General Heller gave the opening charges for the counts of murder against James, and General Tallon presented his counterreasoning as to why all the charges of murder should be dropped, based on no eyewitnesses or concrete proof that the highly preposterous charges were even real. The president of the board called for a recess and the seven members went into the private room that had been reserved as their chambers. The panel had been behind closed doors for less than twenty minutes when the door opened. The expression on Major General Koch's face was grim. He glanced at Colonel Chan, the law officer, and received a curt nod of assurance.

"Gentlemen . . . we have met in closed session and all of us agree that unless the trial lawyer can produce more substantial evidence, the charges under Article 118 will have to be dropped." General Koch wouldn't look Heller directly in the eyes.

Sergeant First Class Colorado rested his eyes on Spencer. He couldn't get out of his mind the scars the young soldier bore all over his body. Colorado's eyes slipped over to the light blue ribbon on Spencer's chest that had five tiny white stars. The senior NCO read the ribbons from the Medal of Honor down to the campaign and service ribbons. The expression on his face didn't change.

Brigadier General Heller slowly stood up behind his table and pushed back his chair using his legs. "Sir . . . I can produce an eyewitness to three of Specialist Mohammed James's executions of American soldiers in combat."

Tallon paused, knowing that what the general had just said would cause a furor in the courtroom. He had guessed right. It took General Koch and five of the MPs to calm the courtroom down before Koch could speak.

"Please, present your eyewitness then, General Heller." Koch used a white handkerchief to mop the sweat off his brow in the air-conditioned room. He had truly hoped that the charges for murder would have been dropped.

"Why didn't you inform us that you had a witness?" Tallon was enraged and beat the top of his table with his fist.

Heller smiled. "After the attempt at breaking James out of Fort Leavenworth and the attempted murder of three of our trial witnesses, we thought absolute secrecy was essential for this soldier's welfare." Heller added before Tallon could interrupt, "The decision was approved by the attorney general's office as legal." Heller turned toward a man dressed in a civilian suit, who had been waiting next to the door, and nodded. The man left the courtroom and returned seconds later escorting a black soldier, who was followed by two men carrying commando M-16s.

Specialist James recognized the man the instant he walked through the doors. Sweat broke out over James's forehead and his left hand started shaking. James wasn't suffering from fear but extreme anger. He should have blown the black motherfucker away when he had killed the rest of the son-of-a-bitch's squad.

"Do you know him?" The bass voice of the civilian lawyer echoed in James's ear.

"Yes."

"From where?"

"I let him live because he was *black!*".

"Did he *see* anything?" The black lawyer felt his shoulders slump even though he tried to prevent it from happening.

"I don't know."

The black soldier wearing a First Cavalry Division shoulder patch took his place next to the witness stand and swore in. He kept looking over at James and the group of black lawyers. The soldier looked confused and Tallon locked in on that.

"Would you please state your name and your unit for the benefit of this court," Heller opened the questioning.

"Private First Class Taylor Barker, Second Squad, Third Platoon, Bravo Company . . ." The soldier lost his train of thought when his eyes locked with James's and missed his battalion. ". . . Second Brigade . . . First Cavalry Division."

Heller saw the glare James was throwing at the black witness and realized that James was trying to break down the man's will to testify against a black brother in court. "Private Barker . . . would you please relate to this court what happened on April fifteenth of this year while you were on a combat patrol."

The black soldier broke away from James's stare. "Yes sir! My squad was assigned to recon an area to the west of our battalion's position. We had set up a claymore ambush and had spent the whole night out there without hearing or seeing anything. When morning came . . ."

"Please continue," Heller prodded the black soldier. "Remember why you are here today."

The soldier broke the eye lock again and started talking. "We were just about ready to break down the ambush when this black soldier just walks out of the jungle."

"Can you identify this black soldier? Is he in this room?" Heller's voice was commanding.

"Yes sir."

"Please point him out to the members of the board."

Barker slowly raised his hand and pointed directly at James. The soldier's finger shook but he held his arm up and spoke. "It was him."

"Are you sure?" Heller needed a positive identification.

"Absolutely. He talked to me and told me to take off after he had shot my squad leader in the back of the head and two more of my squad." The black soldier stood up and his voice rose. "What do you think I am!" He was yelling at James. "They were my *buddies!*"

James sprang to his feet. "They were devilbeasts!"

"Fuck you!" Barker started moving toward James with a murderous gleam in his eyes. "One of those *white* devilbeasts saved my ass from being blown away . . . and another one of those *devilbeasts* paid my mother's rent last Christmas so my family wouldn't be evicted from our home by our *black* landlord!" Barker's voice rose to a scream. "You're the fucking devil!"

"You're *dead*! Do you hear me, motherfucker! *Dead!*"

Four MPs grabbed James and forced him back into his chair. Another pair of MPs escorted Barker back to the witness stand and stood next to him.

"One more outbreak like that, young man, and you'll be charged!" Koch said to Barker.

"I apologize, sir. It won't happen again. . . . But just *seeing him* set me off."

"All right, Private Barker . . . As best as you can, take your time and tell us exactly what happened on that day." Heller knew that he had already won.

"He came out of the jungle and surprised all of us. My squad leader called over to him and it looked like he—James—was as surprised to see us as we were to see him out there in the middle of nowhere. He talked with my squad leader for a few minutes and told him that he had been separated from his unit and was lost."

"How was Specialist James dressed?"

"Like us . . ."

"Please explain exactly how that was."

"Jungle fatigues, backpack, web gear, M-16 rifle . . ."

Barker looked puzzled. "Like us . . . an American soldier."

"Thank you, Private . . . that's exactly what we wanted to hear. He was dressed exactly like an *American* soldier." Heller looked at General Koch. "Sir, I would like to note here for the record that Specialist James was listed as missing in action at that time and as a prisoner of war."

"It's been noted." Koch cleared his throat.

"Please continue . . ." Heller sat down again.

"Anyway . . . James talked to my squad leader and then we were ordered to break down the ambush because James told him that he had just come from the west and hadn't seen any sign of any NVA." Barker looked over at James and clenched his jaws. "That lying bastard was *with* them! He shot three of my squad, and my sergeant tried to zap him but he killed him first. The NVA hit us hard and—"

"Excuse me, Barker . . . what happened *first*—James killing the American soldiers, or the NVA attacking?" Heller wanted the story to fit Barker's statement.

Barker frowned and then looked up again at the trial counsel. "The NVA opened fire . . . that's what gave James the chance to shoot my *buddies* . . . but my squad leader saw him do it and then he said something to James and James killed him."

"And then what happened?"

"James tied a red armband around his arm"—Barker used his hand to show on his right upper arm where the bandanna had been tied—"and then he started moving through the grass until he ran into me. He asked me if I had seen *anything* and I told him no."

"Why did you say that?"

"Because he had the drop on me and I knew that he would kill me if I said yes."

"Then what happened?"

"He looked at me real funny and then told me to get my ass out of there quick."

"Why do you think James didn't kill you?"

Barker's forehead wrinkled and he shook his head slowly from side to side. "I've spent a lot of time thinking about that question and the only answer that I can come up with is be cause I'm black."

"That's *right*, you Oreo motherfucker! If I would have known then that you were a fucking traitor to the black race, I would have blown your ass away too!" James had lost control of himself and was trying to climb over the top of the table to get to Barker.

"Come on, you fucking black Cong! I'll tear your fucking face off!" Barker crouched and waited for James.

"Remove them!" General Koch barked the order. He hit the desk with his gavel. "This court is adjourned until nine A.M. tomorrow!"

The doors opened and a squad of MPs entered carrying a straitjacket and a stretcher.

Brigadier General Heller turned around and glanced at Corporal Barnett. Spencer was smiling at James, who was being held in his seat by two huge MPs while the rest of them tried slipping the straitjacket over his arms.

Brigadier General Tallon looked over at the black lawyer with the bass voice and shook his head. The black lawyer ignored the military lawyer and glared down at James.

The courtroom was being cleared by the military policemen and was almost empty when James was secured in the straitjacket. A team of FBI agents holding exposed Uzi submachine guns stood in a loose circle around Spencer, Arnason, and Woods. They weren't taking any chances on the outburst being a diversion so a hit man could kill their witnesses, even inside the secure courtroom.

James tried spitting at one of the MPs and stopped when his eyes locked onto Barnett standing less than ten feet away, staring at him.

"You're dead!" He screamed so loud, the words were almost indistinguishable.

Spencer smiled. "I hope you're having a bad day, James."

CHAPTER EIGHT

Cold Teeth

The canary-yellow Seville was parked outside the motel-room door in the rear section of the Heart of Fayetteville. The large motel located just outside of Fort Bragg was very popular as a transient billet for military families and as a place for the young paratroopers to go on the weekends and party. The military families were put in the front portion of the motel and the paratroopers were given rooms in the back section where they could party and pick up hookers.

Sergeant Colorado pulled off Bragg Boulevard and parked him GMC truck under the roof in front of the main desk. He looked around the area before he got out of his truck and entered the lobby. He asked the desk clerk for Moore's room and was directed to the back units of the motel. A light misting rain mixed with the road grime on the windshield and Colorado pushed his washer lever to clean the light coating off his windshield, causing the splattered bugs to make it even worse. He pushed the lever again and cleaned the window enough to see as he drove slowly to the back of the long rows of rooms, looking for the number the clerk had given him. The light was burned out next to Moore's scarred door but Colorado located the room by bracketing it with the room numbers on each side of it. He left his truck and knocked lightly. A door opened three rooms down from where he was standing and a very drunk paratrooper wearing only a pair of highly polished jump boots stepped outside holding a bottle of rye whiskey at his side. He looked up at the dark sky and called back into the room, "Yep! It's fucking raining!" Someone yelled something back to him that Colorado couldn't hear and the paratrooper laughed and yelled back, "Have you ever fucked in the rain?"

The door in front of Colorado opened slightly and a thick voice whispered, "Yeah?"

"Sergeant Colorado . . . we were supposed to meet here today."

"Can you come back later?"

"It's fucking raining outside!"

"Just a minute . . . " The door closed.

Colorado pulled up his collar and tried getting as close to the closed door as possible to keep the rain from soaking through his light summer pants. He could hear a chain sliding in a door lock and then the door opened slowly to the dark room. A small nightlight was burning above the bed, but Moore had pulled a pillowcase over it to make the light very dim. Colorado could smell the acid-sweet odor of marijuana in the room.

"I've a *friend* . . . " Moore smiled, "in the bathroom." He nodded toward the closed door. "I'd appreciate it if you could make it short."

"I plan on it." Sergeant Colorado was a trained recon man. His Indian eyes scanned the room as he talked. He knew that he was taking a great risk by meeting with Moore, but the telephone call he had received from Detroit the day before had given him no options. He didn't like the way the events had turned, and the easy money for his ranch was rapidly turning into very difficult blood money. The only thing that had kept him from telling the Black Muslim minister to go to hell was the bonus he was offered, large enough to stock the ranch with top-quality cattle.

"Do you have the uniform?" Moore lit a joint and inhaled deeply as he waited for Colorado's answer.

"Do you have to smoke that shit while I'm in here?" Colorado set the small suitcase down on the bed. A price tag was still attached to the handle. "I've got to return to the base tonight and I don't need for anyone to smell that shit on me!"

Moore glared at Colorado and set the joint down in an ashtray. "Let's see what you've got."

Colorado opened the case and pulled out a folded fatigue shirt that had been starched and pressed by a laundry. "Everything in there is according to the sizes they gave me over the telephone. Don't wear that helmet liner until you leave in the jeep. The MPs in the Eighty-second are a cliquey bunch and one of them might challenge you."

Red Wolf Moore nodded.

"I'll stop by to pick you up at five. . . ."

"In the fucking morning?"

"Yes, in the morning. We have to be out at Camp McCall by seven. I want to make sure we're not late."

"Did you bring photographs?"

"Yes." Sergeant Colorado pointed at the manila envelope tucked under the fatigue pants.

Red Wolf Moore nodded.

"The trial is just about over with. . . . " Colorado was glad. It had been going on for over a week, and ever since the testimony of PFC Barker from the First Cavalry Division, James's chances of having the charges against him dropped were almost nonexistent. "Tomorrow or the day after, they plan on sentencing him, and the board is leaning toward a *death* sentence."

"The black communities would riot across the country if they did that!" Moore was enraged.

"Right now I don't think they give a damn. If what they've proved James has done is true . . . he deserves death." Colorado watched Moore's eyes.

"Whose side are you on?"

"Your Elijah fella is paying the bills . . . right now."

"*Master* Elijah to you!"

"No. He's *your* master. He's my employer." Colorado started turning to leave when the bathroom door opened and a young white male in his early twenties stepped out.

"Is it all right to come out now? Has he gone?" The voice was extremely effeminate. "I just can't wait any longer!"

Colorado could see that the homosexual was supporting a partial erection under the silk lace panties he was wearing.

"Get back in there!" Moore's voice was filled with embarrassment.

"Remember . . . five in the morning." Sergeant Colorado turned to leave. He reached for the door handle.

"If you tell anyone what you saw, I'll kill you." Moore hissed the words out between his teeth.

Colorado used his free hand to reach under his jacket and remove his pistol from his waistband. He turned around slowly and held the weapon at gut level. "When do you plan on doing that?"

Moore's eyes opened wide.

"You're letting your mouth overload your black ass." Colorado pulled back the hammer, using his thumb.

"I was kidding, man . . . just kidding around."

"Watch out that you don't get the clap . . . from him . . . her? Whatever it is." Colorado left the room. He could hear a slap and a high-pitched scream through the thin wooden door. A large man wearing a long beard stepped out of the shadows and started walking rapidly toward Colorado, who was getting into his GMC truck. "He's in there."

The homo's pimp used his shoulder to break the door lock and enter the room.

Colorado smiled as he drove away. Maybe Moore wouldn't be around at five in the morning to ride with him out to Camp McCall.

Sergeant Colorado thought about Arnason and Barnett as he drove down the wet strip back to Fort Bragg. He had served with Arnason at Bragg when they were both new privates fresh out of basic training; he had liked the man. But Barnett bothered him a lot. He had watched the young soldier throughout the whole trial and couldn't quite figure him out. From the testimony the general court-martial board had heard, Spencer should hate James beyond any human ability to reason, yet the soldier sat calmly throughout the whole process and the only emotion he showed was an occasional smile. Colorado was beginning to like the corporal and was glad that James's outburst in the courtroom had tightened security around Barnett so much that he couldn't make the hit he had been paid to make. The Supreme Minister in Detroit was furious, but the lawyer had supported what he had said about the extreme levels of security where even a suicide assassination attempt would have failed.

Colorado passed the World War II paratrooper statue holding the Thompson .45 caliber machine gun under his arm and nodded at the bronze warrior in a silent salute. The road forked off to Smoke Bomb Hill with the main road leading to the center of the large military base. Colorado stayed on the main road and drove straight over to the senior officers' BOQ across from the stucco Officers' Club.

The military policeman on guard at the main door nodded in recognition of the sergeant when he entered. "Still raining out there, Sergeant?"

Colorado nodded and started walking toward his room.

"Sarge . . . the general is over at the Officers' Club and would like you to join him. He told me to tell you if you came in before midnight."

Colorado looked at his watch: it was only eleven o'clock. "Thanks." He went to his room and dried his hair and face before changing shirts and going across the street to the waiting general.

The main entrance to the club was packed with people waiting under the green canopy for their cars. Most of the waiting people were women. Colorado squeezed past them and up the stairs. He didn't know his way around the Officers' Club and looked for a waiter. "Excuse me . . . could you tell me where Major General Koch is?"

The waiter shrugged. "The only place that's open is the main bar upstairs." The waiter pointed toward an arched doorway.

Colorado saw Koch and three other members of the court-martial board sitting around a table in a corner away from the crowd around the bar. The general saw him enter and waved him over.

"Thanks for stopping by, Sergeant Colorado. Have a seat." Koch motioned with his hand. "Would you like a drink?"

"Yes, please . . . double shot of tequila without ice." Colorado needed a stiff drink.

"So how do you like Fayetteville?" Koch smiled and answered the questioning look on Colorado's face. "The MP at the BOQ desk told me. He said that he had overheard you mentioning that you were going downtown."

Colorado nodded. "I just went for a ride. I used to be stationed here years ago."

"Has it changed much?"

Colorado shook his head. "Not much."

Colonel Sinclair and Brigadier General Seacourt were both watching Colorado's face. Sergeant Majòr Thomas glanced around the room, checking for anyone who might be paying too much attention to their conversation.

"I really didn't want to bother you. I know that you've got to get up early in the morning, but I just wanted to alert you that all of the board members have been given a bodyguard by the CID . . . Criminal Investigations Division."

"When did this start, sir?" Colorado tried hiding the fear in his voice.

Koch paused before answering. "It hasn't started yet . . . but it should be in effect by the time the trial starts in the morning. I think they're going to meet us at Camp McCall." Koch frowned. "Have you been threatened?"

"No . . . just curious."

"Good. I thought they were going overboard, but after the two attempts to free James and kill the witnesses, I don't think anybody wants to take any chances during the sentencing process." Koch looked over his shoulder. He knew that he shouldn't be talking about the trial in the bar area.

A waitress brought Colorado's drink and he swallowed it all in one long gulp. "Ah . . . that's the *only* way to drink tequila!"

Colonel Sinclair smiled and didn't say anything. He had caught the look in Colorado's eyes when the general had mentioned the bodyguard. Something was not piecing itself together.

Specialist James sat in his cell. He was in a rage. The Brotherhood was supposed to be helping him and things were getting worse every day. He had done what the Death Angels' code required but they weren't keeping up their side of the bargain. He had gone beyond killing devilbeasts for the mosque and had even sent large sums of money back to the Supreme Minister from the drug operations in Vietnam. He knew that it had been his job to kill white soldiers, but the hundreds of thousands of dollars he had shipped back was a bonus and should mean something to the minister.

The rain pattered against the wood-and-asphalt roof. The soft sound usually was comforting to the human ear, but to James it was a form of torture. He started pacing his cell, making his two military police guards nervous. James had made a reputation for himself with the guards as being unpredictable.

The door to the prison building opened and the black lawyer accompanied by only one other lawyer from Detroit entered the large area outside the single cell. The expression on his face told James that the news the high-paid lawyer had for him was not good.

The MPs opened James's cell and allowed the two lawyers to enter after searching both of them thoroughly for weapons. The senior lawyer had protested the searches but had been overruled by the military.

"Well!" James growled out the word and looked out his window at the rain.

"We've lost the case." The black lawyer didn't mince his words. "We tried and we've lost."

James spun around. "Not *we* . . . brother—*you*! I haven't lost yet!"

"I'll rephrase it for you." The words coming out of the lawyer's mouth were slightly garbled. "*You* lost, and you know what's required from you."

"Fuck you!"

The lawyer who accompanied the senior lawyer from Detroit spoke up. "I can do it for you." The glare in the man's eyes was beyond a threat: it was the statement of a fact.

The senior lawyer looked over at the guards and saw that they were both watching everything going on inside the cell. He coughed and reached into his back pocket for a handkerchief. He used his tongue to shift the metal capsule that contained the cyanide tablet to the front of his mouth and coughed again. He pushed the tablet into the handkerchief with his tongue and casually rested his closed hand against James's bunk, where he released the capsule in the folds of the blanket.

Suddenly they heard the sound of keys rattling and the steel cell door opened. Four hugh MPs rushed into the confined area and pushed the two lawyers up against the wall. A sergeant went over to the bed and brushed his hand over the folds in the blanket until he revealed the bright stainless-steel capsule. He pulled open the two parts and exposed the deadly cyanide pill.

"What's this? A cough tablet, counselor?" The sergeant held out the pill.

The lawyer glared at the military policeman.

Sergeant David Woods sat by himself at the table in the mess hall. All the other tables still had their chairs turned upside down on them. He sat sideways in his chair with his legs crossed out in front of him. David's thoughts were on his family. He was feeling very homesick and lonely. He had been back in the States for over a week and still hadn't seen his parents. He had talked to them three times on the telephone, but it wasn't the same as seeing them. The war had had more of an effect on him than he had thought it had. In a way he was glad that he had spent a week with Arnason and Barnett, away from the rest of his friends. As he sat there sipping his cup of black coffee his thoughts went to those men who were shipped directly from Vietnam back to the States; almost all of them were automatically on leave when they reached the States. He didn't know how they could adjust from the war to peacetime so fast. Within forty-eight hours a soldier could go from a major battle where he was killing people and fighting for his own life, to the arms of his wife or girlfriend. It didn't make sense, and those leaders in the Army who had set up the rotation-and-discharge system definitely had never served in combat, or they would have established stateside holding areas where soldiers would spend a couple of weeks adjusting to peacetime activities.

"I've been looking for you." Spencer pushed back a chair and sat down, followed closely by Arnason. "You got up early this morning."

Arnason paused next to the table. "Sick?"

"Naw, I couldn't sleep." David adjusted his position on his chair. "I'm a little homesick."

"Oh . . . Where did you find the coffee?" Arnason looked back toward the kitchen.

"The night baker made a pot."

"Do you want a cup, Spence?" Arnason started walking over to the serving line.

"Yeah . . . with a little cream." Spencer turned his attention to David. "At least you have somewhere to be homesick about."

"After the trial is over, would you like to come back to

Lincoln with me for a couple of days?" Woods wasn't sure that Spencer would find it exciting enough. "We could do a little bird hunting and some decent fishing with my dad."

"I'd love it! That is, if they'll ever release me from that damn hospital and let me get away from the shrinks!"

"Good! Then it's a date. I'll call back home tonight and tell them the good news!"

"Are you sure my coming along will be good news?" Spencer was worried that he might not really be wanted.

"I've written letters back to them from Vietnam about you guys. Believe me, they feel that they already know you." Woods frowned. "Besides, I'd feel better if you were there."

"Why?" Spencer was puzzled.

Arnason set the brown plastic cup down in front of Spencer and took a seat. He had heard the last few sentences and already understood what was bothering Woods.

"I feel funny . . . about being back here. It's like I don't . . . don't *belong* here, especially without a weapon nearby." Woods glanced over at Arnason. He knew they had the silenced pistols, but he was referring to his CAR-15.

"I felt like that the first couple of weeks I was in the hospital. They thought that I was crazier than shit and wanted me to take therapy, so I stopped mentioning it to the shrinks." Spencer huffed. "I stopped mentioning *everything* to them!"

"I know how you're feeling." Arnason's voice was comforting. "We all go through it. Like we've entered a *nonreal* world when we get off the airplane in California . . ."

"Yeah—exactly!" Woods pulled his chair closer to the table. "Man, I feel naked without my CAR-15!"

"You're not alone. . . . A lot of guys come back here directly from the field in Vietnam and their wives and kids think the guy is nuts!" Arnason lifted his coffee cup to his lips. "The Army personnel system has really let the Vietnam vets down during this war."

Spencer sipped his coffee and made a face. "This tastes like it's been in the pot all night!"

"Yeah, isn't it good?" Arnason drained his coffee and started getting up to get another cup.

"Spence is coming back to Nebraska with me after the trial." Woods was feeling better by the minute. He saw the left-out look in Arnason's eyes and quickly added, "You're more than welcome to join us. We have a huge house and I know my parents would enjoy meeting you."

Arnason shook his head. "I think I'd better look up my ex-wife and visit my kids . . . it's been four years." He went back to the kitchen and returned with a funny look in his eyes. "I wonder what they look like."

Spencer and Woods were smart enough not to say anything.

Arnason concentrated on his coffee cup for a couple of minutes and then looked up at Woods. "I might meet you guys in Nebraska on my way back to 'Nam."

"Sounds good." Woods set his cup back down on the table. "We'd better eat." The sound of eggs being fried on the grill made him hungry.

"Let's do that and then get over to the courtroom. Today is going to be a very big day!" Spencer was the first one to leave the table and grab a tray. He was starved.

Sergeant Colorado had left the officers' BOQ where all the general court-martial board members were staying and walked over to the XVIII Corps motor pool before the first rays of sunlight broke over the buildings. The jeep was waiting for him just as the minister from Detroit had said it would be. Colorado was beginning to really wonder just how large this black organization was. It seemed they had their fingers into everything in the military.

Red Wolf Moore was waiting for him in front of the motel lobby when he pulled up, wearing a complete 82nd Airborne Division's military policeman's uniform. Colorado was surprised. He was expecting to have to wait for the black civilian from Detroit.

Red Wolf seemed nervous and rushed over to the jeep. "Follow me." He didn't wait for Colorado to answer and left the jeep. He ran over to a canary-yellow Cadillac and put it in gear, burning rubber as he left the parking lot.

Sergeant Colorado followed the luxury car down Bragg Boulevard until they came to shopping mall and Moore pulled off the road. He drove behind the mall and parked his car in an empty slot in front of an apartment building.

"Remember the name of these apartments." Red Wolf Moore took over driving the jeep.

"The King George Apartments . . ." Colorado shook his head, "not a hard name to remember."

"Yeah, well, I've got to come back here to get my car."

"Why didn't you just leave your car at the Heart of Fayetteville?"

"Don't ask so fucking many questions!" Moore ground the gears, trying to shift out of second without using the clutch. "You're being paid to supply me with the things that I need . . . after fucking up your part of the deal."

"We'll see how fucking cocky you are once we get out to Camp McCall and you have the opportunity to see for yourself how tight the security is out there."

"You're a fucking *novice*." Red Wolf spit out the words.

Sergeant Colorado leaned back against the jeep seat and pulled up the collar of his lightweight jacket to keep the cool morning breeze off his neck.

The guards at the gate recognized Sergeant Colorado and didn't question his MP escort driving him. The XVIII Corps markings on the bumper of the jeep didn't raise any curiosity either, because it was a common practice to draw vehicles out of the Corps motor pool when the division was overcommitted. Moore dropped Colorado off in front of the courtroom building and disappeared without even nodding at the sergeant.

Colorado walked up the steps and opened the entrance door. His eyes locked with Sergeant Arnason's.

"Hello . . . Red Sleeves . . . it's been quite a while since we've had a chance to talk . . . with you being on the board and all."

Sergeant Colorado smiled; not too many people knew that the word *Colorado* was an Indian word meaning "red sleeves." "I wanted to talk to you earlier, but I didn't want to risk compromising my position on the board. We still have to be careful."

"I understand." Arnason had seen the look on the jeep driver's face when he had stopped to let Colorado out in front of the building. "That MP who dropped you off looked mighty pissed at you."

"Really?" Colorado hadn't caught the look Moore had flashed at him.

"Are you still running recon in 'Nam?" Colorado changed the subject.

"Yeah . . . I've got the best recon team in the country."

"You always were good at training them."

"A lot has to do with the spirit of the men you get."

Colorado nodded. "Like that kid Barnett."

"He's one of the best!"

"Good man?" Colorado's voice lowered just a bit, but Arnason caught the difference.

"*The* best."

Spencer and Woods stepped through the doors leading from the courtroom just as Colorado had asked the question and Arnason had answered. Spencer asked, "*What's* the best?"

Arnason smiled. "Oriental pussy."

"*Wrong!*" Spencer hooded his eyes. "I'm partial to round-eye pussy myself."

"What do you know about pussy, Spencer? You've been laid only twice in your life!" Woods cuffed the back of Spencer's head.

Spencer pointed his finger at Woods. "I've just about had enough of your shit . . . boy!"

"Ignore them, Colorado . . . they should be going into puberty pretty soon!" Arnason grabbed the sergeant's elbow and led him away from the two grab-assing soldiers.

"They really are close, aren't they?" Colorado looked back over his shoulder.

"War buddies . . . closer than brothers." Arnason leaned his rear end against the low ledge of the bank of French windows. "Are you going back to 'Nam soon?"

Colorado shook his head slowly from side to side. He spoke to Arnason, but his eyes were locked on the two highly decorated soldiers. "No, I've put in my retirement papers."

"You've got twenty in already?" Arnason was surprised because Colorado looked too young to be retiring from the Army.

"Got me a small ranch that I'm looking forward to working." Colorado's eyes switched from the soldiers to the black MP standing outside holding a dark blue gym bag.

One of the trial lawyers was standing at the far end of the open waiting area drinking a cup of machine coffee. He had a small portable radio with him that he had set on the narrow window ledge so that he could listen to the morning news while he drank his coffee and ate a honey bun. The announcer's voice filled the long covered porch:

> "This morning the Fayetteville police were called to the Heart of Fayetteville motel . . . the scene of a brutal double murder. A well-known Fayetteville pimp and one of his homosexual hookers were found mutilated in one of the rooms this morning. The police are looking for a black male suspect in his midtwenties, six foot tall and weighing one hundred and sixty pounds. . . . The suspect used the name of Spencer Barnett when he signed into the motel yesterday. . . ."

Spencer's head snapped toward the radio when he heard his name over the air.

"Weird shit." Woods frowned and looked at Arnason.

Colorado swallowed, reached over, and laid his hand on Arnason's shoulder. "We've got to talk, my friend."

The members of the general court-martial board entered the room in single file for the reading of the charges and the sentencing of Specialist Mohammed James. Sergeant Colorado was still a member of the board. The FBI and the CIA both thought that to remove him now would alert everyone that something was wrong, and they wanted the assassin to expose himself. No one was sure that Moore and Colorado were the only two people assigned to kill Spencer Barnett and, now, Mohammed James.

Major General Koch was visibly nervous when he look his seat. The building had been surrounded by infantrymen from the paratrooper company that had been held in reserve, and dogs had been called in to search the whole building for bombs.

Spencer and Woods sat in the same seats that they had occupied for the whole trial; both of them had insisted on staying and listening to the reading of the charges and the sentencing of James. The general understood how much it meant to Barnett and to General Garibaldi to see justice performed and had agreed to their staying in the courtroom

Colonel Chan reviewed the official papers, making sure

that everything was legal, and handed the package back to the court clerk for the reading.

The courtroom was absolutely quiet as the charges and the findings were read. The reporters wrote rapidly on their pads as the charges were covered. James had been found guilty on all counts under Articles 104, aiding the enemy; 105, misconduct as a prisoner; and 106, spying. The clerk looked up and took a deep breath before continuing, "Specialist Mohammed James has been found guilty of murder in three of the twenty-three charges against him under Article 118."

A soft buzz spread across the courtroom and stopped just as suddenly as it had started when General Koch hit his gavel on the table. "Quiet!"

James glared at the general sitting behind the long conference table. He would like just one minute in private with the pompous honkie, just one minute alone! He turned his head and looked over to where Barnett was sitting and saw that Spencer had a look of *pity* in his eyes. Anger boiled into every cell in James's body. He could handle hate, but not *pity*, coming from a white man.

Major General Koch's voice penetrated the red-hate veil that was forming around James's body. "Specialist James . . . do you have anything to say to the general court-martial board before we read your sentence?"

James heard his own voice speaking from somewhere outside his body. He struggled to his feet and tried shifting the ankle and wrist chains so that he could stand more comfortably. "Yes . . . I did everything you have accused me of, and . . . I have done even more! You devilbeasts can't stop the black race this time!"

The black lawyer tried grabbing James's arm to pull him back down in his seat. *"Shut up!"* he hissed.

James glared down at his Muslim-hired lawyer and then spit in his face. "White-trained monkey!"

The lawyer started to reach for James's throat and was restrained by a pair of MPs. *"You are dead! . . . Wherever they put you, James. . . . You are dead!"* He was dragged out of the courtroom.

James continued, "I am a Death Angel!" He turned to look in the direction of Spencer Barnett but his eyes didn't focus. "I've killed twenty-three devilbeasts and I will kill more! Go ahead and put me in your fucking prison . . . I'll kill devil-beasts in there!"

The media was having a field day. Reporters were holding up their microphones to get James's words recorded and the two television stations present were taping the whole event.

"I am a Death Angel!"

One of the other black lawyers from Detroit pulled a long-bladed knife out of his briefcase and thrust it toward James but was prevented from reaching him by an MP's nightstick crashing down against his forearm.

General Koch hit the table with his gavel and yelled above the noise, "Clear this courtroom of everyone except James and his defense attorney . . . and the trial counsels"—he looked over at Colonel Chan—"and the law officer."

The MPs had started escorting the press and the spectators out of the building when the whole back of the courtroom turned into a ball of flame. The blast pushed the massed people back against one another and the chairs in the room. The whole back wall of the building disappeared in a ball of flame. Arnason reacted instinctively and covered Spencer with his own body. Woods had been knocked backward out of his chair and lay semiconscious on the floor.

James's reaction was automatic. He dove toward the MP sergeant who had the keys to his chains. James had watched the NCO put the small keys in the right front pocket of his fatigue pants. It took James only a few seconds to remove his restraints and grab the Army-issue .45 out of the sergeant's holster. James didn't hesitate: he jumped through the burning hole that used to be the back wall of the courtroom.

Spencer pushed Arnason's body off him and struggled to his feet. He saw Woods on the floor and saw that he was breathing. Arnason had a four-foot-long piece of wood siding sticking out of his back. Spencer turned in time to see James leaping through the flames.

Red Wolf Moore stood behind the jeep-mounted M-60 machine gun and sprayed the area around the courtroom. The infantry company had assumed that because there were so many of them and the MPs had secured the whole Camp McCall area, there was no need even to load their weapons. The error was disastrous. Soldiers were dying by the dozens.

There was no place for them to take cover. Red Wolf was laughing as he raked the ranks of paratroopers with the deadly fire from the machine gun. The first belt of ammunition was used up in seconds. He reached down to load another 250-round belt, giving the infantry company commander a chance to fire his .45 caliber pistol. The first round went through Red Wolf's cheek and lodged against his upper teeth. He turned and stared at the man who dared shoot him and then growled. His hand slammed down the cover on the machine gun. The second round hit him in his chest and he slumped over the black-painted weapon, streaking his blood on the hot barrel. The smell of his own blood baking reached his nostrils first. The captain fired again and Red Wolf dropped down on his knees, his fingers fighting to reach the trigger of his weapon. The captain ran over to the side of the MP gun jeep and emptied his pistol into the body of the Death Angel.

"You fucking bastard! You bastard! . . . You bastard!" The captain dropped to his knees and held his hands up to his face to hide his tears. "You . . . fucking bastard!"

James ran through the smoke and found himself up against the perimeter fence that separated Camp McCall from the swamp that surrounded a portion of the Special Forces training area. He stepped over to one of the steel posts that supported the Cyclone fence with the row of concertina wire that had been recently strung along the top. He didn't hesitate and reached up with his hand to lift the wire off the post. The engineers who had laid the wire had been under a lot of pressure to get the job done, and in their rush they hadn't tied the wire down to the support posts. The concertina bounced, fell off the top of the fence, and hit the ground. James dropped down off the top of the fence and pushed himself away from the pole so that he wouldn't land on the wire. He remained crouched on the pine needles and sand while he oriented himself. The infantry guards had not bothered setting up outposts in the swamp because they didn't think anyone would risk trying to infiltrate through the snakes, quicksand and mud.

Spencer saw James climb the fence and started running toward him. When he saw the handle of the .45 sticking out of

James's belt, he dropped to the ground, then ducked behind a building and watched to see which direction James would take.

James disappeared into the thick stand of pine trees that circled the edge of the marsh area leading into the swamp.

Spencer searched the area around him for a weapon and saw none. He had to move fast or he would lose James. He ran over to where James had scaled the fence and pulled himself to the top before pausing to look back toward the courtroom. The whole area was in a state of confusion. Spencer heard the steady fire coming from an M-60 machine gun and thought that the gunner needed lessons on how to fire the weapon. As he dropped down to the ground and started running toward the woods, he was breathing heavily and the cool air he inhaled made his teeth cold. Spencer closed his mouth and felt for a second the coolness against his front teeth before he smiled. He might get his wish and be able to tear James's throat out with his teeth. They were the only weapons he had with him as he disappeared into the North Carolina swamp.

CHAPTER NINE

Sharp Teeth

Spencer became the ultimate recon man the instant he touched the shadows of the thick stand of trees. He was dressed in a set of short-sleeved khakis that were already mud covered. He paused next to a shallow stream and checked the banks for the direction James had taken. The broken branches of a large purple loosestrife plant that overhung the stream gave Spencer the information he needed. The bees circling the purple flowers gave Spencer additional information: James had only recently passed the plant. Spencer scooped up handfuls of the black mud that bordered the sandy stream bottom and rubbed the thick paste over his bare arms and around his neck to keep the hordes of mosquitoes away. Spencer smiled to himself and used three fingers on each of his hands to mark streaks of mud warpaint on his cheeks before taking off to follow James.

Major General Garibaldi was the first one to recover from the explosion in the courtroom after James and Spencer had left. He saw the weathered piece of siding sticking out of Arnason and knew instantly that the sergeant was dead. Woods was shaking his head, trying to clear his vision. The whole court-martial board was lying on the floor, and the loud chatter from a light machine gun outside the building kept the occupants kissing the polished floor. Garibaldi scooted over to Woods and lifted his chin with his index finger. "You all right, son?"

Woods nodded. "Yeah. . . . How about—" He saw Arnason lying on the floor. "Sarge!"

Garibaldi grabbed Woods's shoulders. "He's dead, son."

"*No!*" Woods tore away from the general and struggled to his sergeant's side. "Oh *no!* He survived Vietnam to die here?"

Major General Garibaldi understood what Woods was saying and nodded sadly in agreement. It was very ironic.

The sound of the machine gun stopped outside the building and the low-frequency popping sound of a .45 replaced it.

Woods suddenly stopped trying to shake Arnason awake and looked around the courtroom. His eyes were filled with panic. "Spencer! *Spencer!*"

Garibaldi instantly joined Woods and began searching the rubble for Spencer.

"*Spencer!*" Woods ran to the hole in the back of the building and stepped outside. "*Spencer!*"

James slowed his pace. He knew that if someone had seen him leave the camp, they would have opened fire or tried to follow him. He smiled to himself. He was free. All he had to do was remain calm and work his way out of the swamp and then hitchhike back to Detroit. He had a lot of debts to pay back. James stopped walking. The stream bottom began to get deeper suddenly as the shallow stream joined up with a wider flow of water. He looked for dry land but couldn't see any except for the dense clumps of undergrowth that bordered the waterway. He decided on wading across the wide-open, stump-filled expanse of water to what looked like a decent-sized island that was covered with tall loblolly pines. The water reached his midchest before it began receding again. He was glad, because he really didn't want to have to dog paddle in the brackish water.

James was about ten feet from the island when the water roiled about twenty meters away. A five-foot alligator made its escape into the swamp lagoon.

"Fuck!" James tried running out of the bog and tripped over the submerged roots of long-dead trees. He fell face first into the brown water and rose almost instantly at a full run. He didn't stop until he was a dozen feet up on dry land and then whirled around, holding the .45 out toward the water. "Motherfucker!" He was angry and embarrassed over being afraid of the alligator. James stood up and screamed, *"Motherfucker!"*

Spencer stepped out from the overhanging bushes that bordered the stream entrance to the swamp lagoon just as James screamed at the alligator. He saw James exactly at the same instant as James saw him.

The .45 echoed against the trees. A large hunk of rotting wood tore loose from a dead tree a foot above Spencer's head as he stepped back under cover.

James didn't need to be told who the man was wearing the filthy khakis. He knew almost instinctively that it was Barnett.

"Come on! Come on, motherfucker!" James fired two more rounds at the spot where Spencer had disappeared.

There was no way that he could cross the swamp lagoon now that James had seen him, so Spencer backtrailed for a hundred meters and broke through the underbrush. Less than fifty meters from the stream, the ground started to rise and dry out. Spencer turned to his left and started jogging between the trees and low shrubs. He heard a couple of wild pigs grunt and escape into the bushes to his right. A large oak tree occupied a small clearing where the pigs had been feeding on acorns. Spencer grabbed a low limb and started climbing as fast as he could up the trunk. The climbing was made easy because of the huge limbs and sparse leaves on the old tree. He stopped climbing when he was high enough to see above the scrub pines. Spencer could see the black column of smoke coming from Camp McCall and the power lines cutting through the high ground of the swamp a mile away. There was a finger of taller pine trees that intersected the power lines from where Spencer sat in the tree. He could hear the occasional sound of a car passing by in the distance and figured that a highway ran parallel to the power lines. James would stay on the high ground and head toward the road. Spencer was almost sure he wouldn't venture back into the swamp. He had served on recon patrols with James and knew how the man operated. James always took the easy way out if given a choice.

Spencer picked a course through the swamp that would intersect with the path James would most likely take and dropped down from the oak tree. He started running at a mountain man's pace to cover the extra distance he needed to circle around and get ahead of James.

The military police and the infantry units took up guard positions around the courtroom building. Red Wolf Moore had killed twelve infantrymen and wounded another thirty-six before he was killed by the captain. The Supreme Minister would have been proud of him, except that he had failed to kill both of his assigned targets.

Major General Koch stepped out of the building and surveyed the carnage. "You mean to tell me that *one* man did all of this?" He couldn't believe what the MP commander had told him.

"Yes sir." The officer was visibly embarrassed. "We weren't prepared for someone attacking from *inside* the camp, sir."

"How did he get in here?"

Mr. Manning, from the FBI, spoke up. "He came in disguised as an MP escort to one of your board members."

"A board member!" Koch was aghast.

"He was briefing us about his involvement when it happened." Mr. Templar, from the CIA, nodded toward the building across the street.

Koch's eyes opened wide. Only one of the board members had been absent—Sergeant First Class Colorado. "He was helping him?"

Templar nodded. "But he had a change of heart and was trying to prevent the slaughter. We still have a lot of good information from Sergeant Colorado about the source of these attacks and I think he's going to be very useful."

"I'll have him court-martialed!" Koch was livid.

"We've already promised him immunity, General. We have to move very fast if we want to break up this operation." Manning tightened his jaws. "The FBI has suspected for a long time what Sergeant Colorado has confirmed for us . . . and it's bigger than what you see here, General—much bigger."

Spencer felt his lungs tighten and a burning sensation in his throat. He wasn't used to running and his hospital stay had not given him the opportunity to develop his stamina, but he wasn't going to let James escape.

James walked fast through the low shrubs over the thick

layer of pine needles. Water oozed out of his shoes, making a sick gushy sound. He held his .45 tightly in his hand and kept looking back over his shoulder.

James whispered to himself, "Come on, motherfucker . . . come on and die!" If he had known that Spencer was unarmed, the chase would have been a short one, but he assumed that Spencer had picked up a weapon before following him.

The ground in front of James dipped but he could see that there was a wide strip of swamp between him and the high ground. James did not like the idea of crossing the waterway, especially after having seen the alligator. He paused and searched the area before taking a slow step into the brackish water. The water was tea colored but he could see the bottom, which made him feel a lot better. James was correct in thinking that the portion of the swamp he was wading through was a large depression in the ground that had been cut off from the rest of the swamp. If he had tried circling the water hole, he would have been able to stay on dry land but he would have had to fight very heavy underbrush. He didn't mind the water as long as he could see the bottom and the area around him as he waded across.

The water reached a little bit above James's crotch as he walked slowly through it. He tried walking on his tiptoes to keep his black pride from getting wet. Psychologically, the idea of his testicles and penis being submerged bothered him.

James looked ahead of him as he walked and saw that the bottom of the water-covered depression was covered with a thick layer of pine needles and decomposing oak leaves. A long, fat object appeared in the corner of his eye and he sucked in a lungful of air. He could see that it was at least ten feet long and wide—very wide. James pointed his pistol and fired three rounds before he caught himself. He was sure that it was a huge alligator swimming along the bottom. He fought the water against his legs and struggled out onto the bank. A shiver traversed his spine and he turned around and fired two more rounds at the submerged beast.

"Fuck you!" He shivered again. "You motherfucking bitch!" His voice was almost hysterical. James stood on the side of the bank and watched as the water calmed down from the impact of the bullets and his passage. The shape of a large, dead tree trunk appeared on the bottom of the tea-colored water.

"Damn you!" James was livid over being tricked and scared by a rotting tree.

Spencer heard the rounds. He paused and thought hard. He was sure that James had fired eight rounds from the Army-issue .45 caliber pistol. The clip held only eight rounds, so unless James had taken extra ammo from the MP, the gun was empty.

Barnett used the echoes from the rounds to locate James's position in the swamp, and he smiled. James was slightly to his left rear, exactly where he wanted him. He would be far enough ahead to cut to his left in a few meters and ambush James.

The tracking dogs sniffed Spencer's T-shirt and bayed. They wanted to get to work. Woods reached over and tried taking the M-16 out of the hands of one of the infantrymen standing nearby.

"Hey! Man . . . you try that again and I'll blow your ass away!" The paratrooper wasn't about to part with his weapon.

"Trooper, give him your rifle," Major General Koch's voice left no room for argument, "and your web gear."

"Yes sir." The paratrooper obeyed.

Woods took the gear. "Thanks . . . That's my buddy out there and I have to help." His voice was apologetic.

"No problem, as long as the general said so." The paratrooper wasn't going to take on a general, and he was happy as long as his honor wasn't fucked with.

The dog handlers unleashed the first two hounds, who shot around to the back of the building and paused only for a couple of seconds before they ran over to the Cyclone fence and started baying next to the pole and the disturbed concertina wire.

"They crossed the fence here." The lead MP waved for an engineer holding a pair of bolt cutters to come over and cut a hole through the fence. They weren't going to waste any time circling the whole camp and then having to walk a couple of miles through the swamp just to reach the same place.

Woods paused as he slipped through the hole in the fence and looked back at the Army ambulance that was loading up Sergeant Arnason's body. He blinked back his tears. There would be plenty of time later to cry. Right now he was going to hunt down and kill James, and God help the man if anything happened to Spencer.

* * *

Spencer paused to listen. The swamp to his left had become quiet. He could hear insects and frogs to his right and behind him, but the area immediately surrounding him and to his left rear was quiet. He was sure that James was far enough to his left rear for him to cut over and get ahead of him.

James had slowed his pace. He was getting very tired. He stopped to rest in an open, sunlit spot on the ground and swatted at a horde of mosquitoes circling his head. The loud sound of a semitruck filled the swamp. James's head snapped around to face the sound. He smiled and jumped up on his feet. He was within a few hundred meters of a road. The sound of the semi gave him renewed strength and he started running in the direction the sound of the truck had come from. James ran up against a solid barrier of brush and thick grass that bordered the wide ditch running parallel to the raised highway. He paused and looked both ways and saw that the thick band of vegetation went in both directions. If he wanted to reach the highway, he would have to break through the brush and wade through the ditch. The sound of a car passing by on the highway only a few meters away made up James's mind for him. He was only a short distance from the road.

Spencer broke out of the brush and saw James's muddy wet tracks on the pine needles. He looked in the direction the footprints pointed and realized that he had just missed him. He didn't allow himself the luxury of becoming angry. Spencer was hunting and he had all his energy concentrated on the spoor of his prey. He searched the area for an ambush and he crouched low to the ground before moving out after James.

The brush was so thick that James couldn't see his feet. He felt the warm water flow over the tops of his low quarter military shoes and realized that he was nearing the flood ditch. He pushed aside the brush and saw the embankment of the highway on the other side of the twenty-foot-wide ditch. He figured that it would be deep and he would have to swim a couple of strokes, but that wouldn't slow him down now that he was so close. James turned his head to look down the ditch but was too late to prevent the coiled six-foot-long cottonmouth from defending its territory from the intruder. It slipped off the log it had been sunning itself on and swam toward the creature who had disturbed its rest.

James saw the huge snake and realized that he could never make it back to dry land before the creature reached him. He locked in on the gleaming eyes as the cottonmouth swam with its head held high above the water.

"Get the fuck away from me!" James pointed his pistol at the snake and pulled the trigger. The click sounded louder in James's ears than it actually was. He screamed and threw the pistol at the reptile. It landed a foot in front of the snake and only made the huge snake madder. It opened its mouth and showed James why it was called a cottonmouth.

Spencer heard James's scream.

The snake bit into James's leg three inches above his knee. James could feel the hot fluid pumping into his flesh. He used his fist to hit the snake's head but succeeded only in pushing more of the deadly venom out of the snake's glands.

Spencer arrived just in time to see the monster snake release its hold on James and swim downstream to another log to finish its sunbathing without being disturbed.

James saw Spencer approaching. *"Help me! Please help me!"* He thrashed the water.

Spencer stopped on the edge of the ditch and watched James struggle through the shallow ditch over to the embankment. The water had looked deeper than it actually was. Spencer looked for the snake before crossing after James. He found the Death Angel lying alongside the asphalt road, breathing heavily.

"Man! Put a tourniquet on my leg! I can feel the poison burning!"

Spencer dropped down in a Vietnamese squat and watched James struggling with his pants leg. He finally gave up and unbuckled his pants. He pulled the black web belt free of its loops and shoved his pants down below his knees. Spencer could see the swelling puncture marks of the cottonmouth's fangs. A little excess venom oozed out of the holes.

"Help me!" James screamed.

Spencer watched.

A car drove past and braked hard, leaving rubber streaks on the hot asphalt. The driver threw the car into reverse and veered off to the side of the highway. He jumped from his car and ran over to where James lay screaming.

"What happened?" He looked first at James and at Spencer, who squatted there watching James die.

"Snakebite! Please help me!" James grabbed the man's leg.

"Sure, son. . . . Let me back my car over here and I'll get you to a hospital."

"Leave him be." Spencer's voice carried so much threatening hate that the man felt a cold rush along his spine.

"Are you crazy?" He felt fear.

"Leave . . . him . . . be."

The man stumbled back toward his car. "I'm going to get the sheriff!" He threw it in gear and drove off down the highway.

"Come back! Don't leave me!" James screamed after the disappearing car. He rolled over onto his stomach and touched the hot road. "Oh! Help me . . ."

A shudder rippled through James's body. The large dose of venom had started reaching his heart. He opened and closed his mouth in an involuntary muscle contraction.

Spencer remained squatting there, staring at James. He heard the sound of dogs baying back in the swamp and turned his head slightly toward the ditch. He saw the fat six-foot cottonmouth curled up in the crook of a huge log and stood up with a handful of small rocks he had picked up from the side of the road.

"Git!" Spencer threw a rock at the snake. It landed about a foot in front of the log. The cottonmouth raised its head off its coils and stuck out its tongue to sense the air. Spencer threw another rock and it bounced off a small branch on the log. The vibration from the rock got the snake moving into the water. It started swimming toward Spencer. He threw another rock in front of the reptile and it changed direction.

"You aren't very smart for as big as you are!" Spencer chucked a couple of more rocks at the retreating cottonmouth.

The first dog broke through the underbrush and entered the water. She swam directly over to the side of the ditch Spencer was on and crawled out. She took one long sniff of Spencer, threw back her head, and bayed.

Spencer patted his leg. "Come here, girl." He made a clicking noise with his tongue. The hound stopped baying and nuzzled his head. Spencer looked over at James and saw that he was going into convulsions.

The brush parted and Woods broke through the undergrowth with his M-16 held ready to fire. Sweat streaked his face and saturated his khaki uniform. He had stayed behind the dogs and was a good three hundred meters ahead of the rest of the patrol.

"Yo . . . David . . . up here." Spencer waved to his teammate.

"You all right?" Woods gasped for breath.

"Yeah. Hurry up or you'll miss it!" Spencer waved for Woods to run.

"Shit! I'm fucking dead!"

"Then you won't feel the pain. Hurry up!" Spencer squatted again and scratched the dog behind her ears. She moaned with the pleasure the human hand brought her.

Woods struggled up the steep bank and saw James lying next to the road. "What happened?"

"Snakebite." Spencer nodded downstream at the still-visible cottonmouth swimming slowly away.

James gagged and vomited.

"Shouldn't we do something for him, Spence?" Woods didn't like just watching and doing nothing, even for James.

"I am." Spence smiled. "I'm watching him die an *easy* death." He reached over and pulled a stem off a clump of wild grass and carefully cleaned it before slipping it between his teeth.

Dear Mom and Dad,

Well the trial is over and things are pretty much getting back to normal. Spence is fine and will be heading back with me.

You know sometimes things really got a little hairy, but we always made it through, and now that Spence and I are back together the Viet Cong better watch out.

Your loving son,
David